DOWN A BREAK

Tim Mullane

Enjoy the
read! Tim Mullane

DOWN A BREAK

ACKNOWLEDGEMENTS

My gratitude goes out to all who spent time with me between the lines in those Santa Fe days. It wasn't just about teaching tennis. It was always much, much more.

Being down a break means nothing more than that you have an opportunity.
—Lanny Bedford, "The Long Hard Court."

Do you want to find out who you really are? Only pain can tell you. The kind of pain you find between the lines. What is tennis if not a metaphor for life? The lessons of pain and joy that one finds on the battlefield of tennis are deeply intertwined with the mysteries of life.
—At The Public Courts: Conversations with the Professor, alias "The Pusher."

...Lanny scrambled back looking up directly into the blazing sun, desperately trying to see the ball through the sun snakes in his eyes. Leaping off his back foot he launched his tall, muscular frame into a scissors kick. He reached up hoping the ball would be there, and snapped his wrist. Blinded, he couldn't see where his overhead landed. His father's immediate roar of approval sounding above the cries of the spectators told him it was good. Relieved, he bent over hands on his knees, his sides heaving. Sweat poured off his face and dropped onto the wooden frame of his Dunlop racket. He watched the drops create a little pool beneath him.

"Come on, Lanny!" his father shouted to him. "Suck it up! You're right there!"

He could almost feel the court boiling under his feet. Feeling dizzy, he tried to catch his breath.

How, he thought, *can I breathe so hard and not get any air?*

The last few games he realized had nothing to do with tennis. He had stopped thinking about strategy, about the score, about his opponent. His understanding about how to work a point flashed in and out of his awareness like a distant beacon. He didn't know what the hell was going on. He tried to reach inside his mind and grab hold of his concentration but it slipped out of his weakening grasp. An instinct deep inside him told him to go forward, forward, get in, get in tight to the net. COME IN ON ANYTHING!

He glanced at the big clock next to the court. He could see that the match was past the three-hour mark. He had never played so many deuce points in his life, had never hit so many overheads. This wasn't tennis, he thought to himself, but some sort of strange, grueling, Roman arena game without bloodshed. But mentally, he was bleeding. He straightened up and staggered slightly. His feet felt completely raw. The blisters started at the beginning of the third set. Every split-step, and every time he planted his weight sent stinging pain through him. His hamstrings quivered on the verge of cramping. The lone voice in his head that said: *I can't,* soon joined a chorus of *you can't, we can't. Where are all these voices coming from?* Every part of his body that pained him had a voice. Looking up he seemed to see things in slow motion. His ears were clogged with sweat and all he could hear was his labored breathing. He remembered his father telling him that once you start fighting yourself you can't fight your opponent.

And Lanny remembered that match where he whined, threw tantrums and pouted to a 0 and 1 loss to a kid he should have beaten easily. After the match his father asked him what happened and he said weakly: "The kid just played better than me."

His father grabbed him by the shoulders and looked directly into his eyes.

"Do you really believe that crap? You just got your ass kicked and the only thing you can say is that he just played better than you did?"
His father's face grew into a tight grimace and he shook his head.

"You gave up, didn't you? You quit, didn't you?"
"No, he—"
"Don't lie." His father cut in, giving his shoulders a shake. "Don't lie to yourself. Son, what in the hell do you think tennis is?"

His father's glare made Lanny look down. "I don't know." Lanny squirmed in his father's grasp. "It's tennis. It's a game, isn't it?" he managed with a pout in his voice.

Paul Bedford gave his son a long searching look. "Tennis is a fight," he said flatly. "That is what tennis is: a fight," and his father emphasized this with a shake of his fist. "Never," his father continued, his eyes blazing, "never be a traitor to yourself. Never! I don't care about your pain, your fatigue, and your frustration.

Nobody does. Never betray yourself. If I see you play another match like you did today I am through with you. You're on your own."

Lanny reeled under the impact of those words. His twelve-year old chest contracted with pain and he almost fell when his father released him. The memory of what his father had said to him still stung.

How can I be thinking of that at this time!

He shook his head and wiped his forehead. He could see his father in the stands, face beet-red with emotion, yelling, pumping his fist at him. But all he could think about was getting off the court. He didn't care what happened. He just wanted it to be over. But once the point started an animal instinct took over pushing aside his pain and exhaustion for another point and then another. In between points he bent over, gritted his teeth and sucked in air.

I have nothing left, he thought, *nothing.*

He wanted his body to make him quit. There would be no betrayal in that. No shame in that especially the way he had been playing and everybody could see that the conditions were horribly hot and grueling. No shame.

Yeah, no shame, he thought in a whisper of conspiracy. *But if you lose,* another voice whispered, *you'll be a loser. It doesn't matter what happened before or after—you'll be a loser. No, it won't be like that. The conditions got the better of me. What could I do? The blisters! The cramping! The damn sun always in my eyes! And this guy, he doesn't play tennis. All he does is lob!* Rationalizations bounced around in his mind like a tennis ball gone mad.

What's all the shouting about? He heard himself say in his mind. He felt a stitch in his side and tried to rub it out.

The crowd was on its feet clapping. He could recognize his supporters. There was his friend John White. He had beaten John in the last round. *Ah, poor John, he could never beat me but that never got in the way of our friendship. He's a good guy.* There he was gritting his big teeth, trying to transmit his intensity to Lanny.

Those people cheering, Lanny thought, *they don't know what the hell* I'm *feeling. They've got no clue.*

And if they did, he reasoned, they would be silent. His father would look at him kindly and say it's all right to stop now. No need to go on. But on they went yelling and cheering, wanting and needing—*oh, my dad wants me to win so badly. God, just look at him!* And he bent over once more, putting his hands on his knees.

Sure his supporters had carried him but now he almost felt angry with them. He wanted to yell at them to shut up and let him be. Let him have some peace to get his breath back, which seemed to have left him two games ago. The wall loomed large in front of him. Another couple of steps and he would hit it.

He had run out to a 4-1 lead in the third set. But his opponent, Justin Lucchi, a whipcord of a kid with tireless legs and a permanent annoying smirk had steeled himself, grinding out point after point with games going to deuce six and seven times. He ran down every volley Lanny punched into the corners and pulled out every lob in the book. And he lobbed and he lobbed high into the overhead sun. After losing a point by framing an overhead Lanny looked over at Lucchi and thought: *I can't fight the sun and this bastard at the same time.* His opponent read his mind and flashed a fierce grin and chuckled under his breath.

After an hour into the third set Lanny was on serve 4-5, and serving at break point at the USTA 18s National Junior Championships at Kalamazoo. His stomach felt queasy with fatigue and dehydration. He thought for a moment how absurd it all was: *All that work to get to this point!* All the countless sweat-filled hours of practice, the easy victories and the long gut-wrenching losses. How could all that time be defined by this horribly short moment?

He felt a quick surge of rage and fought down the impulse to spike his racquet on the ground. *This is not fair!* A voice screamed in his head. He shook his head and droplets of sweat dropped on his shoulders. All of a sudden he knew that what happened next could change him into something else. Would the little kid hitting a new tennis ball against the wall until it became bald, be remembered? Would he still be the little kid who won the match but cried in frustration at all the errors he made during a 1 and 1 victory? Would he remember how, in the beginning, he just wanted to make his father happy—then, *had* to make him happy?

Lanny bounced the ball, preparing to serve realizing how quiet everything had turned. The sound of the bouncing ball was so loud it almost echoed in his ears. He would do what he was born to do: serve-and-volley. There was no way he could summon up the strength to go for a hard flat one down the T. And he had no desire to see if he could come up with a good second serve. He was going to spin it in and then close in tight. A deep breath and a grunt of pain and off he went trying to get to the service line before he had to split-step. Expecting a hard return off his serve he got a floater instead. A FLOATER!!!!

... Again *that* volley... Lanny jerked awake and sat up. Again he could hear that the rain had started again. He wiped his sweaty forehead and breathed deep trying to calm his pounding heart. That volley came to him in his dreams, in different matches, on different surfaces, with the same soul-shattering result: "OUT!" It wasn't just any volley, oh, no. It had defined him, shaping him with the power of fate and inexorable destiny. Somewhere, in the corner of the first clay court of tennis, that call had had been written.

That volley. He had stoned it pure and simple. He could still see the seams of the ball, its beautiful yellow felt as it sat up for him, above the net, like a willing sacrifice. But something alien entered his hand. A dark heavy force spread throughout his palm and fingers smothering all the feel and sensitivity that had gave him, in the eyes of his opponents and coaches everywhere, the best volley they had ever seen in the junior ranks. "OUT!" It was over. *It was really over.* He remembered glancing quickly over to his father and saw his face twisted with anger, disappointment and pain. His father's look went through him like a bullet. Lanny had collapsed onto his back, relief and sadness pouring over him…

"OUT!"

Lanny laid back down on his side pulling the covers up to his chin and stared into the darkness of his bedroom. In the stillness just before dawn, when the merging of night and day create an opening to the past, Lanny could hear the "out" call that resounded from the corners of the quiet house. Out went his life that day. But most of all out went his feel for the ball; a unique and mysterious feel that he could not describe to anyone without the risk of being laughed at or dismissed. Twenty-two years had passed burying the memory of his lost feel into a vault deep within him; twenty-two years since he had lost in the finals of the National 18s Junior Championships in Kalamazoo. Often he had tried to conjure up that lost feel as if it were a long-ago-lover that had touched him in a way that made his body vibrate with the force of a heated heart. But it never came back to him. The feel was gone.

He had loved the ball. He loved the way it came over the net to him. He loved the way it caressed his strings; the way it challenged him, and yes, punished him; above all, though, he loved the way it made his hand feel, inviting him to do as he pleased with power and mastery...He had loved the ball.

Sighing, the memory of it all still immediate and painful, he rolled over in bed. The mattress springs seemed to groan for him. He glanced over at the picture of his ex-wife that he kept on his nightstand. *My ex-wife,* he thought. *What a strange sound: My ex-wife ... my ex-companion, my ex-friend, my ex-lover ... or just my ex. Surely it will shorten to that over time.*

And of course he was an "ex": an ex-tennis player, and ex-son, an ex-husband, ex-companion… So that is how it goes, he mused. You live your life accumulating "ex's". And when you have enough "ex's" you've lived long enough: death is really the last "ex" that you can experience.

How could I have let her go? He asked himself bitterly. *Oh Yeah, I remember. I lost the feeling for her, the same way I lost the feeling for the ball... It just left one day. But I was happy, wasn't I? No... Maybe I was just comfortable. No, it was just a convenient place to be in... Damn these thoughts! I don't know what happened.*

How can all he thought he had loved and had spent so much time loving, he wondered, just vanish in a day? What a horrible instability had lain at the root of all he thought was stable. He heard the rain coming down. *That's strange*, he thought. It never rained at this time of year. For a second he considered the message that had been left on his answering machine yesterday. He hadn't answered his phone for the last week but he did listen to his messages.

Why talk when you have nothing to say? Words are useless, he thought. *All those therapy sessions and the talking, the talking, the expressions of feelings: How do you feel about this and that. Jesus, how many feelings can one person have?* He almost scoffed out loud to himself.

If you constantly stir up the shit in your life, he reasoned to himself, well, than sure enough, your life is about shit. Hell, there is mud at the bottom of everyone's life but for Christ's sake, there are plenty of rivers with muddy bottoms. But, from the surface down, they are clear as a bell!

He tried to push these thoughts aside as he replayed in his mind, a message that was on his answering machine this morning. What a voice out of the past! It was an old friend from his junior tennis days, John White. John said he had called "your father... Yeah, he's still crusty as ever..." "The old man said you both still haven't talked in about twenty years...man, that's some crazy shit..." blah, blah, blah. And "hey, now that you have nothing in your life..."blah, blah. "Why don't you come out to Santa Fe and work at the club with me. I am sure you'd be a better tennis teacher than—what the hell is it you teach? English as a third language? Some shit like that?" Blah, blah. "Don't be a loser. Come on out." Blah, blah.

John was always a blowhard, Lanny remembered. But it was true. There was nothing in his life. He enjoyed teaching English and philosophy classes at the community college but he could do that anywhere. Santa Fe, New Mexico. Man, that was really out of the way, he mused with interest, but certainly out of the way was where he was headed. Perhaps he could just pick up and leave. Perhaps he should. His life here had a bad karmic feel to it now. But he wouldn't be going out to Santa Fe to teach tennis to a bunch of hacking club players. That's the last thing he wanted to do. Tennis should be played one way and all the rest is a waste of time. Tennis was the muddy bottom of his river and he didn't want to stir it up. Santa Fe would just be a place he was going to. He didn't intend to arrive anywhere.

He sighed deeply and hoped the rhythmic pattering of the rain on the roof would call him off to a sleep he desperately wanted and needed, a respite from the pain of the present. He had to stop the wounds of the past from reopening. But his memories persisted...

After that loss at Kalamazoo he felt fear and the ball knew it. He began to play from the back of the court, against his instincts, serving himself up for slaughter to the baseline bashers who pounded him mercilessly. His father stopped watching him and would just drop him off at the tournaments, telling him to play with his heart. What a disappointment he could no longer play for his father...

Lifting his right hand he looked at it, looking for his old hand but seeing again the alien hand with that dark heavy force lurking in the soft tissue of his palm. *The feel. It's gone*, he thought. *Forever.*

He remembered when he began to withdraw from serious competition. The gunslinger in him was blinking. His hand could no longer pull the trigger smoothly. His racket felt like a club. He couldn't get the hard stare back. Soon, he made peace with this new reality.

Rather too easily, he thought, remembering how quickly he had let go, losing match after match. He felt that there was nothing he could have done about it. He just watched himself being swept away from tennis.

While Lanny had accepted that tennis would no longer be in his life, his father, Paul Bedford, could not. Paul Bedford thought his son was supposed to accomplish great things, he was going to be a world-class tennis player. Paul had grown up on the public courts developing a game that was all heart. Nicknamed "Scrappy," Paul scratched and clawed for every point. Often a match with Scrappy felt like a fistfight. Scrappy scraped his elbows and knees all over the court, leaving the hard surface marked up like a clay court. Coming from a poor family Paul taught himself how to play by playing. He had never drilled in his life, only played. Devoid of technique, Scrappy had an ugly, ruthless game. He didn't win matches. He survived them. But his son would learn impeccable technique and develop beautiful fluid strokes for all to admire. His son would not grind it out from the baseline, spitting back everything that came over the net, absorbing everyone's big hits, but would play a classic serve-and-volley style, attacking and overwhelming, a display as Paul put it, of beautiful violence."

Rolling over on his other side seeking a comfort he couldn't find, he realized just how empty his bed felt: cold and empty. She had left two weeks ago. He was teaching the morning she left. Ironically as he remembered, he was teaching a class dealing with Shakespeare's sonnets. And he imagined that while she stuffed all her personal belongings into boxes and threw away wedding pictures, he was reading part of a sonnet to the class. Part of the sonnet said:

> *Let me not to the marriage of true minds*
> *Admit impediments. Love is not love*
> *Which alters when it alteration finds*
> *Or bends with the remover to remove.*
> *O, no! it is an ever-fixed mark*
> *That looks on tempests and is never*
> *shaken; ...*

Obviously he and his wife's love had been shaken, Lanny acknowledged that, though it hadn't taken a tempest.

He pulled a pillow close to him and he could still smell her body's essence of feminine warmth, like warm milk sweetened with a slight pinch of cinnamon. Reflexively, he breathed deeply trying to pick up a scent of her sex that he remembered was like the smell of fresh seawater in a tide pool.

No, that smell was long gone, he knew. They had stopped making real love six months ago, but occasionally they did come together. Deep in the middle of the night when unconsciously, an arm or a leg reached out across the emotional void between them and touched off a primal need to satisfy a desperation that only their bodies felt. Entwined by pure instinct, rather than love and affection, these raw bodily moments allowed them the chance to hold on to something while everything was falling apart.

Ah, the succor of sex, he thought, *how those times would have been totally unbearable without those few moments when we could forget our pain. And then, to wake up the next morning sharing that...that conspiracy of silence, God...what we're capable of.*

Lanny thought a lot about his father lately. They hadn't seen each other after he quit competitive tennis and went off to college. He paid his own way while earning two master's degrees in English and philosophy without a note of congratulations from his father.

It's been about twenty years and I will never forget his sad, angry face, Lanny thought bitterly to himself. *He never understood me. I wanted to stop. To get off the goddamn train that was killing me. He wanted to drag me down with him in all his disappointment. Why should he be disappointed? He never lost one point or one damn match. He never lost his guts on the court or played with blood flowing around toes from blisters the size of quarters. What the hell could he have suffered? Well, there was my mother. But what has that got to do with me? I guess it will always have something to do with me.*

Lanny felt his eyes burn. *What a miracle of life I was; some kind of angel of death I was.* Lanny tossed and turned. The sound of the rain provided no solace.

Over twenty years now, he thought. *You're an ex-son... get used to it.*

He ran away. Yes, he ran away. To put his father's sad, angry face a million miles behind him and his last words: "You have ruined my life. Everything I've done has been for you. All the lessons, the miles, the driving, the hours and hours we spent together on the court. I loved it. I would have sacrificed my life for it. And now, you want to throw it away. You're nothing but a coward. A coward. If it weren't for you, my wife would still be with me, loving me...holding me."

The pain of those words still burned in Lanny's heart. Every time he thought he might call or write his father, his father's last words turned his mouth grim, his wounds opening again. All they had had was each other. Lanny's mother died in a car accident while driving to the hospital. Pregnant with Lanny, her water broke early and her labor began hard and excruciating. Driving home from her sister's house in the country, on that gray morning in 1961, in the driving rain, she lost control of the car. Lanny was removed from her dead body.

Lanny's father never remarried, putting all his love and devotion into his son. There would be no other woman for him. The memory of his wife's skin on his, the smell of her neck, the way they made love, and how she whispered to him while they were in bed would not be diminished by another. As long as the warmth and weight of her presence lay against him at night he was content. He could speak softly to her, telling her of their son's progress on the court and how great he would become.

Lanny again rolled onto his side drawing his six-foot frame together into a fetal position. He thought he would like to be a baby: knowing nothing but a soft breast, knowing nothing of loss. At forty, Lanny knew what life was about. It was about loss. He had never felt a mother's nurturing kiss or been able to seek a child's solace in her arms....*" If it weren't for you my wife would still be with me, loving me...holding me...."* He could never get rid of the thought that yes he had been responsible for his mother's death.

My life for her life? He still agonized over why it had been that way, especially every time he looked at her picture and saw the features that exactly resembled his: the smooth forehead punctuated by a widow's peak; high cheek bones, a stronger version of his mother's mouth, and eyes that had the deepest shade of blue; all crowned by tawny colored hair that had highlights of yellow. The only difference being the masculine square line of Lanny's jaw from which sprouted a closely cropped goatee in which a couple of stubborn gray hairs could be seen.

My life for her life? he thought again. *No way I would have allowed that if I could have. And look, mother, what a legacy*

was plucked from your dead womb. How proud you would be of me, he thought derisively. *No, if there had been a way...*
He couldn't escape that thought: *I'm responsible.* Certainly no one would agree with him and his sensible mind told him so, but in that part of his heart where he remained a child he couldn't agree. And hadn't his father said so?

Lanny breathed deep, yawned and rubbed his eyes as if trying to rub out the past. Again, he looked at the picture of his wife-no his ex-wife on the table next to the bed. His look turned perplexed then wistful. He was still confused about it all. He expected to see her walk in at any time and say wow, what a mistake she had made and could he forgive her. No, that would never happen. He shook his head wondering why he could even think that. Eight years of marriage, all the closeness, but he never really knew her. Many times he thought she would act one way and she ended up doing something else which always surprised him. He wanted her to be a certain way and she wanted him to be a certain way and so they went their own ways.

But what was wrong with my way? he thought, shaking his head, trying to clear the complexity of it all from his mind.

Towards the end the silence grew loud and filled the ever-growing space between them. How bizarre, he thought to himself. All the coming together, the love, the shared intimacy, the hopes and dreams and then...the growing apart, emotions being peeled back until the void lay bare in front of both of them. Another loss. It seemed as if his world had rolled under him like a great whale going belly up.

He carried the puzzling pieces of his failed marriage around in his head, continually trying to reconstruct them into a whole picture, to understand what had happened. How—towards the end—could it have unraveled so quickly? He felt like a stranger looking at his own life. He thought things had been going along fine and then one night, as they lay in bed after making love, his wife, in a whisper, said that she was unhappy. Flush with contentment of his loving exertions he heard but didn't hear her soft words. He patted her leg and rolled over.

What a cost silence comes with, he now thought.

At first he just couldn't accept that his wife was unhappy. She didn't have a right, after all *he* was happy—or was he just content? She should be happy too. It doesn't make sense. He couldn't believe her then and he didn't now. To do so made him feel false, a fake, a fraud of love. Yeah, that's what she made him feel like: a fraud. She fell into that hole inside him that his mother had created.

He felt sad. The rain on the roof sounded like the thousand tears of his life coming down. He wanted to feel sad. He thought he should be crying. He tried but nothing came from his empty dry eyes. Summoning up his deepest sense of loneliness and regret he tried again...Nothing. He sighed with shame and watched the second hand of the clock tick around the dial. Outside the rain suddenly stopped and a dry wind kicked up swiftly and blew up harshly against his bedroom window. The wind made a sound that he could hear in the middle of the night, coming from the barren, badlands, deep in the far corner of his heart, a wind that had dried up his eyes perhaps for good. He had no tears. He never did. For men without mothers there are no tears.

Exhausted, he slowly drifted off to a fitful sleep, and of course, into the dream he didn't want to have.

*I admit it without hesitation: my son was my life. My wife died
tragically. I was so heart-broken, grief-stricken, and yes, I was
furious, furious that she had left me with the coming of my son.
I raged, shook my fist, wept in the middle of the day—all kinds of
mourning. It smothered me. But—God help me—I blamed my son.
Sometimes I would hear him crying in his crib and I would hesitate
for a moment while I thought of my pain. Oh, Jesus. Jesus. He was
here and my wife wasn't. I felt such shame over that. I resolved to
dedicate my life to him and he would never know, never suspect
that I, at one time, had blamed him for his mother's death. Sure I
had wanted to let loose and medicate myself with booze, divert
myself with cheap sex. Grief is a tough opponent. It can break you
down and make you betray yourself. I could have been a mess. But
I did what I had to do. Obviously, I am not God's gift to coaching
but there is one thing I tried to teach my son and that was not to do
what he wanted to do on the court but do what he had to do. Just
like in life. Being a mature tennis player or a mature person is the
same: you do what you have to do. Was I hard on him? Yes, but
only as much as my love would allow. Of course I have regrets and
most of all I regret that I wanted...I wanted too much for him to
succeed. I never thought to ask him how much he wanted to
succeed. I thought it was a given. I thought my will would just push
him along. I think it was too much for him to bear, ultimately. Did
he quit? I never asked him that exactly. When he pulled back I felt
the pain of defeat. My loss. I had failed. Poor me. Even the
passing of time has not diminished the disgust I feel over how
selfish I had been, but yet something inside of me—and how
terrible it is—is still bitter and disappointed... And now in the
pained silence between us I feel nothing but compassion and
sadness for my son. But by God he could have been great! What a
beautiful game! Such a volley! I tell you what: McEnroe was only
an equal in that department. I still tremble with what could have
been. During all of his junior years, I never asked him how he felt.
I just saw a kid, a tennis prodigy with a gift for the game of tennis
that could have only been given by God. And he was my son! When
I failed with my son I also failed the memory of my wife. What is*

there left for me? Life is most bitter when you think you deserve something.
—Paul Bedford, "Notes To My Son."

He had to leave. And fast. Yes, he was going somewhere but it didn't really matter where. Just go. All night Lanny packed boxes and threw out memento after memento as if trying to unburden himself. He had no desire to sleep another night in *that* house.

He and his wife had completed their business so quickly.

A simple dissolution. The words couldn't form on his lips.

That's what they had agreed upon. They had no debts together, no mortgage, no children, no future to barter over. Hell, they could part like friends, like business partners…like polite strangers. They split their savings. At the end of the meeting she cocked her head sideways and looked at him. She had never looked at him that way. He quickly offered to pay the seventy-five dollar filing fee. And that was that.

A simple dissolution: the final words of a marriage, of our eight years together. How simple, he ironically thought to himself.

She had left some of her stuff: stockings, cosmetics, a pair of pajamas, a hairbrush full of her fine blond hair that he rubbed between his fingers for a moment. All of this she left behind for him to add to the trash, perhaps to send him the message that he, in his ways, had thrown it all away. The rent had been paid, the house cleaned, although some stains could not be removed no matter how hard he scrubbed.

Lanny made a last round through the house, wandering from room to room like a ghost, the sound of his almost weightless footsteps echoed off the bare walls and came back to him as if from a great distance. Bare. His life lay bare before him, a bare page where words had been slowly erased. His future stretched out before him like a barren path, bare and "unreadable" a psychic friend of his had told him the other day. And of course his heart was bare and as thin and insubstantial as that of a ghost's.

There's nothing left. He hadn't forgotten anything.

I leave nothing behind, he thought. *It's as if I had never been here.*

He looked around. How big the house seemed now that it was empty. No evidence of their life, its promise, its joys and disappointments remained.

It hit him. *Man, there's nothing more final than an empty house.*

He closed the back doors of the U-Haul truck and made sure the lock was secure. He took a quick look to see if his car was secured correctly to the trailer.

A gray front of clouds had crowded down on the beach as he headed out east on the Santa Monica Freeway. *It'll burn off by noon,* he knew, and then realized that that would be the last time he made that comment about the weather.

As he passed over the 405 Freeway and approached downtown it seemed he noticed for the first time the ugly stream of billboards, the fog of smog that hugged the skyscrapers, the endless grid of suburbs and congested streets: a gray concrete web that trapped all who were senseless of their surroundings, all who were willing. He was no longer willing.

The most important thing my father ever taught me in tennis was how to learn to learn tennis. It blows me away to think of how many people have told me that they couldn't learn to play tennis. In effect they said that learning is a talent, you either have it or you don't. If you know how to learn, know what the process requires, you can learn anything: tennis or physics. I know a lot of pros that don't want to make their clients uncomfortable. Well, if you are not uncomfortable, how are you going to learn anything? The learning process is not always fun or immediately gratifying. Many have forgotten the pleasure of resistance, the enjoyment of difficulty, the anxious excitement of initial failure. You can't go at tennis like a consumer. You can't buy tennis with a few lessons. Sorry, you've got to earn it. And repetition is the key. Ah, if people could only realize the genius inherent in repetition.
—Lanny Bedford, "The Long Hard Court."

Lanny had been in Santa Fe a week now. The bare trees that lined the streets showed the city to be deep into the fall season. And he had the sense that there was something odd about the fall here. Can a season feel…old? He wondered to himself. The fall here in Santa Fe felt and looked old to him. The harsh bareness of the trees, the dull gray-brown of the mountains that towered above the city seemed to suggest that it had been years since the green and bright colors of spring led their charge across the landscape.

As he crested the hill on highway 285 that led down into Santa Fe he thought how small the city seemed nestled up against the mountains and not a skyscraper in sight. What would he use for a frame of reference as he moved around the city? As he looked off to his left he saw the national cemetery, a rolling hill of perfect white tombstones and he thought that the neat rows of graves and the organizational nature of such cemeteries always offended him in a way that he couldn't articulate. Over the hill of tombstones he could see the great stone Catholic Cathedral of St. Francis of Assisi which seemed to dominate the city's skyline, and it struck him as quaint—a kind of seventeenth century feeling as he remembered from looking at pictures and sketches of European towns in the seventeenth century where churches, not bank buildings or even governmental buildings, were the biggest and most prominent of a city's center.

Well, he thought, translating to himself: *Santa Fe, city of holy faith. In a city with that name a church should be the tallest building.*

He made his way down St. Francis Drive turned left onto Agua Fria toward downtown and then turned right onto Guadalupe. Paying attention to his directions he really didn't observe too closely his surroundings, but finally an impression bubbled up as he pulled into the parking lot of Dominic's restaurant.

Damn, this town is brown, he thought to himself. *Brown homes. Brown buildings. What's with all this brown?* Somewhere in his memory he knew why but he couldn't fish it out, though it had to be obvious. He had always considered the color brown to be a common, neutral, elemental color. He wondered if he could lose himself in all that brown and neutralize his life.

Now that's a thought, he figured to himself. *I could be a brown man in a brown town. Hell, I'd be invisible.*

Entering the restaurant he felt a sense of familiarity. The restaurant had old, rough brick walls, track lighting, huge wooden beams supported the ceiling and kitchen utensils decorated the room. A big menu board hung on the wall behind the service counter, and he could hear Billie Holliday singing over the PA system. He heard what he always thought were the greatest lyrics of all:

> *Momma may have, Papa may have,*
> *But God bless the child that's got his own...*
> *That's got his own.*

And I don't got my own, do I? Just carrying my own past. That's it, he mused to himself.

The restaurant reminded him of Main Street in Santa Monica. He looked around and saw a bunch of Anglo faces that could have easily been in any deli on Melrose Avenue or in any bistro in downtown Manhattan. For a brief moment he thought he hadn't traveled over five hundred miles through the emptiest landscapes he had ever seen to a small, way out of the way town, the oldest town of historical significance in America, a deeply Hispanic town that jealously traces its origins to Spain, not Mexico, a city full of muddy history and an adobe permanence that has no glass and steel buildings to reflect a grasping, modern visage. But all that information seemed to be from an old travel brochure as Lanny looked out over the restaurant crowd.

A waving arm caught his attention and he noticed his friend, John White. He hadn't seen John in twenty years. But there was no mistaking the blonde, square-jawed look which now sported a blonde/gray goatee that appeared more like fur than hair, the muscular look, the coiled presence, and those fiercely bright green eyes that always appeared to Lanny to have their own energy source; eyes of—

—*Eyes of a predator! That's it,* Lanny remembered.

John was *the* fastest player Lanny had ever competed against.

He still looks like one big muscle, Lanny thought to himself.

"John, you're a long way from the beach. What happened to your goldie locks?" Lanny said while smiling.

"Yeah, well, I retired from surfing a long time ago. But I've been known to snowboard," John replied, a big grin on his face. "Dude, you look the same. What a trip. I thought you would be old and fat."

They shook hands and embraced, pounding each other on the back.

"No, sorry to disappoint you. I stay in shape. I jog a lot, ride the bike, and I've been lucky enough to keep my hair," Lanny replied.

"You've certainly got that right," and John ran a self-conscious hand though his thinning hair. "Let's sit here." John indicated a booth in the corner. "Hey, I'm sorry to hear about your divorce."

"I'm sorry about it as well," Lanny replied regret in his voice. And he sat down heavily.

"Man, that's a tough one," John commiserated.

"I don't recommend it. But perhaps I deserved it. "

Lanny kept coming to this conclusion more and more. He was never aware of his role in the decline of his marriage, never aware of what his subconscious had—he saw now—clearly set in motion.

"Any tennis?" John tried to change the subject.

"Nope," Lanny said flatly. "Haven't picked up a racquet in about fifteen years."

"Fifteen years! John said in shocked amazement. "No kidding? Man, that's bizarre."

John tugged at his mustache thoughtfully. *This guy was a tennis fanatic. I wonder what happened. I really thought he, of all the guys we grew up with, was going to make it.*

"I remember tennis was everything to you."

"Well, that's all in the past," Lanny managed a mixed motivated grin. "And you? Are you still as fast as a scared rabbit?"

John's eyes blazed as if he had just received a shot of testosterone. "Man, I could still run down any one of your damn volleys and pass you up the line," and John laughed heartily.

Boy, old John's still strung pretty tight, Lanny thought.

"I bet you could."

"Hey, remember that junior tournament—where the hell was it at—oh, yeah, in Pasadena. Remember those junkie courts?

"We were playing on the far court, the one that had the ripped net and that…." Lanny grinned, "that tree."

"That Goddamned tree," John intoned. "I remember it well. That one big frickin' branch that spread out over the deuce side and you kept volleying to that side and when I tried to lob the ball it would hit that damn branch. Oh, man, that pissed me off! Cost me the match, along with all those pussy drop shots you hit. Shit, you were the only kid who hit those droppers. You made me run my ass off."

Lanny listened to John with a growing excitement and then laughed loudly and pounded the table, a glow coming over his face from a source that hadn't been tapped in many years. His heart quickened and he felt a surging sense of physical vitality. He fought down the urge to jump up.

"And remember, you called me an asshole in that…in that squeaky voice of yours," Lanny almost shouted.

"Yeah, and we both stopped and looked around to see if there was anybody watching, because you could get kicked out for swearing on the court. There was always some parent who would go tell the referee. And when you didn't see anybody you—"

"I called you an asshole back," Lanny cut in with glee.

"And we spent that whole third set calling each other every name in the book, " John laughed heartily, his face turning red with mirth and the memory of their outrageous behavior. "Dude, that was fun!"

"And I won," Lanny rubbed it in.

"Yeah, you bastard, you always won," John smiled with mock grimness. "Imagine nowadays getting kicked out of a tournament for swearing. Ha!"

"Yeah," Lanny agreed. "Imagine that."

They both paused for a moment, deep in their memories of all the matches they played against each other. Finally, John sighed:

"Man, you were a player…"

Another pause. Lanny looked out the window off into the distance trying to get some space between him and the past that they both had conjured up, but he could see that court right across the street and could hear their high adolescent voices as they cursed at each other.

Lanny sniffed, having come down as fast as he had gone up, "That was a long time ago, John."

"Yeah…But man, you were, Lan you were." John said lowly, confirming to himself what he felt whole-heartedly… Then he said quickly: "Hey let's order something to eat. I'm starved."

Caught for a second by John's fervor, a door blew open to Lanny's junior days that had been emotionally sealed for years. He felt a momentary flush of how the feeling used to be: the confidence, the swagger, the athleticism of his play, the surge of adrenaline after a big serve and a crisp volley deep into the corner for a winner... *And the feel, oh the feel,* he thought to himself, *the feeling of the ball on my strings as I did whatever I wanted with it.*

And as he started to realize that nothing since came close to equaling the sense of freedom and sheer joy, an arm came out and slowly closed the door. Lanny looked down at his napkin and fiddled with the edges of it.

"Hey, man," John finally broke the silence, "it's good to see you"

Lanny smiled and nodded. "Yeah, you, too."

He seems all right but I can tell he's carrying a load, John thought to himself as Lanny appeared to smile with an effort.

"Hey, I got a place for you," John gushed excitedly. "It's an adobe house, man. It's really cool. The walls are like two feet thick."

"A house of mud, right?" Lanny responded, realizing that that's what the brown was all about.

"Yeah, partner, that's the style here. It's over one hundred and fifty years old. Dig that. At one time, I was told, the most desirable prostitute in town lived and entertained her customers in that house. They called her Miss Lady because while around town she conducted herself like a proper lady. They said she had once been a part of high society back east and had been married to a prominent doctor." John smiled. "And then she showed up in Santa Fe."

"Great. So I'll hear a bunch of ghostly Johns and their horny moans in the middle of the night. Just what I need." Lanny's sour tone made John smile.

"Hey maybe so. Anyway, you need to get some history in your life."

"Hey, in LA there are—"

"Ah, man," John cut him off, "the only thing a hundred and fifty years old in LA is the garbage. This place was made by hand. It's small but cool like I said. It has a kiva, too."

"A kiva? What the hell's that?"

"It's one of those funky little fireplaces. You know, like the Indians used to make."

Funky, thought Lanny. "What's the funky price for this place?"

"The rent is a thousand bucks a month. It's a very good price."

"What? A thousand bucks," Lanny scoffed. "I thought New Mexico would be cheaper than LA."

"Dude, I know you just got here, but Santa Fe is not New Mexico. It just seems like it; you know, like a Hollywood set. It'll take a while but you'll figure it out, especially with that heavy-duty education you've got. You'll love it. Santa Fe's a little town, but it has stuff just like LA."

"Oh, Yeah? Besides the prices?"

"What about this restaurant?" John gestured. "That's why I chose it as a spot for us to meet."

"Ok, it's similar."

And John smirked. "Just like LA, this town has too many real estate agents, lawyers, gay waiters, and wannabe Indians. Hell, you'll feel right at home."

"So, how big is this hundred and fifty year old adobe and where is it?" Lanny asked.

"Oh, I don't know. It has a bedroom and a bath, a kitchen area. I guess about six hundred square feet or so. I mean, what else do you need? And you're in a primo location, just off Canyon Road down a little alley. I have a client who has a studio and next to the studio is this little adobe *casita* that he's not using right now."

"But, John, a thousand bucks and a small place, couldn't I—"

"Look, he could get a lot more money for that little place, believe me," John cut in, spreading out his arms for emphasis and waving them as if he were trying to get airborne. "He's doing me a favor. You're getting a great deal."

John looked at Lanny who still seemed on the fence.

"Hey," and John continued enthusiastically, "Canyon Road is the most famous street in Santa Fe. You'll be able to walk to a lot of cool art galleries and restaurants. Dude, what's with the long face? You'll love it," John said smiling as if he were on the beach, surfboard under his arm.

John will always be that tennis playing and surfer kid from Redondo Beach, no matter how long he's been away, Lanny thought...

Later that day Lanny moved into the little *casita*. Down an alley way just off Canyon Road, and past a few small galleries, the *casita* stood under a huge oak tree that leaned way out over the top of the house as if threatening to fall right down on it. He had never seen a structure like it before and likened it to a small gingerbread house, or something out of a children's fable. There wasn't a straight line or a square edge on the outside or the inside of the house. It seemed to Lanny that it had been crafted on a gigantic clay spinning wheel. Lanny stopped in the little entrance way and looked around.

"What do you think you're standing on?" John asked.

Lanny looked down and stamped his foot testing the hardness of the floor, thinking to himself that it felt hard as a rock.

"Well?" John prompted with a tone that said Lanny wouldn't know.

"It's very hard. I would guess some sort of flagstone or cement."

"Wrong, pal. It's actually the original floor of the house. It's been covered over in the rest of the house with wood floors."

"Okay, so what is it?"

"It's a deer blood and dirt floor. Hard as hell isn't it? The deer blood mixed with dirt, can be as hard as flagstone," John said, proud of his knowledge.

Lanny gave John a funny looked saying in effect: *How the hell did you know that?*

John read Lanny's mind and quipped: "Dude, I just didn't get off the surfboard, you know. I've been in this town awhile. It's interesting. You'll see."

No matter how he struggled, Lanny could only fit half of his furniture in the house. The small confines of the house frustrated him and he felt strangely troubled that he couldn't have more of his things around him. He barked angrily to himself as he tried various arrangements, but to no avail. The *casita* seemed to be forcing him to have only what was necessary. In a sense it was…stripping him.

This place is like a little trap, he thought to himself while he panted with the effort of pushing around the furniture this way and that way. And he felt like he was pushing himself around as well. Resigned, he sat down and caught his breath and let a bitter thought flow through him in a way that he almost enjoyed: *I guess life wants to take everything away from me.*

He loaded up the rest of his furniture and put it in a storage facility off San Mateo. He stopped off at the hardware store and grocery store and settled in for the night. And then it hit him. Over the next four days he never went out. He didn't realize how the forces in his life had led him to Santa Fe and now inside the little house he hit the wall of those forces and he felt the panic of trying to move without going anywhere. He feared to go back and he didn't know how to go forward.

As a kid, his life was structured around tennis and conditioned by the discipline and hard physical work it demanded, coupled by the expectation of high achievement. He had approached academics the same way, going at his studies the way he had gone to the net: relentlessly.

And now, for all his discipline, sense of structure and ordered ways, Lanny felt totally rudderless, without an anchor, bereft of routine and all those predictable tasks that had carried him along during the day. He felt a strange form of paralysis. Just after one o'clock that night he became fully awake and caught himself listening and waiting…for what? And the anxiety: where the hell did that come from? He listened as if waiting for a branch in the jungle to snap, and all he could hear, he thought, were the only heart beats in the universe…and they pounded away in the distance as he drifted back to sleep.

The next night came quickly because he had slept through the whole day not wanting to be awake with his own thoughts. Outside the wind, chilled by the approaching winter, blew dead leaves up against the inset windows and tried to blow hard against the two-foot thick adobe walls in a battle that the wind couldn't win. He was surprised how the temperature dropped so quickly after the sun had set and he could feel the dry, thin air starting to crawl across his skin. He built a fire in the kiva and stared as the orange and yellow flames began to dance inside the fireplace's oval opening, an opening that seemed like a window into a culture of fired kivas, structures made of earth, pounded corn, fry bread, and roasting chile. The dryness reminded him of when he passed through a desert region of Chihuahua during a trip to Mexico and stopped in a small, desolate town that seemed abandoned except for the cantina. After a few lukewarm beers that didn't quench his thirst, Lanny had looked around the dingy, shadow-ridden cantina sprinkled with men in grimy jeans, torn shirts, and sleeveless ponchos, who never looked up from their drinks, as if afraid their beverages would evaporate before their very eyes. Since he had recently been deep into the graduate writing program at UCLA and felt that words came easily to him, he scribbled a poem on a napkin that looked like it had been used before.

As he stared into the Kiva fireplace and watched the evocative flickering flames, the words of his poem came to him as he remembered the title: Silviano's Cantina.

> *Think of it: Beer Warm*
> *As burro piss,*
> *Eyes loaded with*
> *Skeletal barrancas,*
> *Stares that slip*
> *Through open*
> *Windows like*
> *Ghostly crows*
> *Passing the*
> *Dead horizon,*
> *Dry murmurs*
> *Whisper through*
> *Waterless lips,*
> *Whispering hunger*
> *Whispering draught,*
> *Whispering dryness*

That rolls the skin off
A man's back
And falls on the
Dirt floor, like brown
Parchment scrolls,
Telling of a grief too
Barren for tears,
Telling that
Jesus had lived
Nearby, before he
Embraced pain,
And God, having
Spent an accidental
Day here, found
He knew no one,
Lost his voice,
And left unnoticed.
Think of it:
Beer warm
As burro piss,
And where time
Only means the
Waiting for water.

What am I waiting for? He wondered to himself. He
stirred the fire and watched it leap higher and felt a warm glow on
his face. He scratched at the dry patches of skin on his back and sat
down on a chair that leaned up against the wall and stared at the
ceiling above him, a ceiling buttressed by time-worn vigas that
slightly sagged under the burden of history and crisscrossed with
etched and pitted latias. He thought about the countless others who
had looked up at the same ceiling. Had they looked up in pleasure
while being serviced by the famous Miss Lady? Certainly Miss
Lady had looked up into the rustic, handmade ceiling while
thinking of chandeliers and the smooth ivory painted ceilings of
her affluent past. He wondered if Miss Lady's well-to-do and
secure life had suddenly come tumbling down around her, and that

she, like Lanny, had found that she was in the desert of her life. And both of them looked around the open desert and decided that to go in one direction was just as good as another. He turned his head to the adobe wall and put his nose against it. The sweetly thick odor of piñon smoke, the spicy pungency of roasted red and green chiles and boiling posole—odors he would later come to identify—filled his nose like an odorous tapestry. And behind all of it he could recognize the musty earthen smell of old, dried mud.

What exactly would he say when someone asked him why he had come to Santa Fe? He couldn't say he was on a personal quest to find a new spirituality, or to find himself among the cave dwellings in Bandelier, or to heal himself of some karmic disease using the plethora of alternative and non-traditional treatments available seemingly everywhere, or to confirm that he had been an Indian in a former life. No, God didn't send him to Santa Fe and no, he wasn't writing the next great confessional, past-life-regression novel, or creating the next faux Santa Fe style of painting. And he certainly didn't come to teach tennis as his friend, John White had suggested, and in fact, had offered him a job. He didn't really know why he had come to Santa Fe and he didn't care. He hadn't really *decided* to come. He washed up onto the beach of Santa Fe, delivered by the wave that entered his life just before his divorce. Life was just...happening to him.

"So, what brought you to Santa Fe?"

Lanny sat engrossed, looking at the menu with its list of exotic *tapas.* Momentarily he looked up and around the dimly lit bar. The smell of stale beer and cigarette smoke assaulted his nose. He could make out the fading Spanish frescos that decorated the walls. What a funky little dive this El Farol bar is Lanny thought, concluding however that funky in Santa Fe comes with a steep price.

After five days alone with his thoughts and his past he had to get out from behind the adobe walls that seemed to have a need to confine him. He had walked down the little side street to Canyon Road and wandered past the art galleries and concluded—from what art he could see in the gallery windows—that unfortunately, art is what anybody thinks it is and apparently is worth what anybody thinks they should pay for it. And finally, he thought that there seemed to be a lot more hobbyists than artists showing their work on this road. Not everyone's a poet, even if they don't know it, he used to say to his students. Discovering that he was hungry he walked into El Farol.

"I said, what brought you to Santa Fe?" an insistent voice next to him asked. "I can tell you're not a local."

Lanny turned to face his bar stool companion with a look of: Who, me?

The man nodded at Lanny expecting an answer. Lanny took a swig off his Tecate and thought the man looked like some sort of burnt out sixties' hippie or new age type with his gray hair tied back in a ponytail. His skin had the waxy look of someone who takes too many vitamins. His blood shot eyes stared at Lanny, almost daring him to answer, and his toe tapped while he spoke which made him give off a twitchy kind of energy. He certainly wasn't on his first beer. His throat and fingers bristled with turquoise jewelry.

Wow, Lanny thought to himself, *a real new age dandy.* Thinking about what he had done over the past week since he had arrived in Santa Fe, Lanny felt he could offer up an answer.

"I came to Santa Fe for the fast food, the customer service and the high rents."

He thought it novel to go into a store and know the store help didn't care if you bought anything or not, especially if you flipped out your California driver's license when paying with a check. The clerk would roll his or her Hispanic eyes and say to a colleague: "*Otro.*"

"Never heard that one before, but I know what you mean. You sound like a local," and the man chuckled, then downed a shot of tequila. "That's part of the damn small town charm," the man said through smiling eyes that watered from the potency of the tequila.

Competitive tennis is what it is. It is like the universe: it regards us without concern; it offers no promise or danger. Things happen during a match over which we have no control: balls that dribble over the tape, balls that hit the lines, miss-hits that drop in for winners, an ace that rockets by us, a gust of wind that carries a ball long, an opponent who is in the zone. These are realities and you must face them with no, I repeat, no emotion, and the justifications you hear in your head won't help you, but will only weaken you. Accept these realities; let them pass through you, and you will find that either in winning or losing you will discover peace on the court and that peace will fill you with joy, the real joy of tennis.

—At The Public Courts: Conversations with the Professor, alias "The Pusher."

For days Lanny had been waiting for the call. He knew it was coming before the phone rang; he knew what John would ask him, and he knew what he would say but he didn't know that he would be persuaded. For the last two weeks he had slept through mid-day. The stardust the sandman sprinkled in Lanny's eyes at night also contained the heavy grains of emotional exhaustion, depression, and an ever-present past. But last night the heavy-lidded and solemn sandman stayed away. Lanny awoke early and went out to retrieve the newspaper. Snow had fallen during the night and a couple inches of light snow sat perched on the canals and on the rounded lines of the little casita. Again the image of the gingerbread house trimmed with frosting came to his mind.

While laughing at the misspellings and grammar usage in The New Mexican newspaper, the call came.

"Hi John," answered Lanny.

"How the hell did you know it was me? You've got caller ID, don't you?" John asked.

"No, I just knew it was you."

"Man, you must be physic or something."

"About some things, yes," Lanny replied. "You want to ask me to come up to the club and check out the facility."

"Hey, man, you are exactly right. So? How about it?" John asked, a little excitement coming into his voice. "You've been hiding enough in that little adobe of yours. And don't tell me: maybe some other day," John accused.

"Now how did you know that's what I was going to say?" Lanny asked, surprise in his voice.

"Hey, I've seen you once in twenty years. I know how your mind works," John laughed. "Listen, today is just as good as any day. So, come on up."

Lanny opened his mouth and said something different than what he had intended: "You're right. I'll see you later."

The Santa Fe Racquet and Fitness Club, surrounded by a thick piñon forest, nudged up against the base of the Sangre de Cristo Mountains. The club's adobe style building bristled with vigas that protruded from the walls just under the flat roof. To Lanny the building and the club's setting seemed more like a retreat than one of the town's athletic clubs. As Lanny walked through the club's entrance a sign above the doors etched in wood with tendentious lettering said:

Here mind and body are one.

How "Santa Fe" Lanny thought. And then a little voice reminded him that that was true when he was playing his best tennis; there was no dissonant dialogue between his mind and body, only a flowing exchange of instincts that were reflected in the fluidity of his game.

Big leather chairs and southwestern furniture decorated the lobby of the club. It had the relaxed air of a large, informal living room in a hacienda. New Mexican folk art and landscape paintings covered the whitewashed walls. A large kiva fireplace that rose up to the high ceiling painted with deep earth tones, ablaze with piñon logs, dominated one corner. Large cuts of flagstone covered the floor. Huge vigas, two and a half feet in diameter, supported the herringbone cedar ceiling. Some people, their faces still flush from their exercise, sat and talked happily, still feeling the rush of endorphins. Others, particularly the three older men who traded jokes and scratched at the crossword puzzle in the newspaper, Lanny figured, came for the company, not the exercise.

John met Lanny at the front desk. John had his usual strong-toothed smile on and his bright green eyes blazed with energy.

"What do you think?" John asked while he shook Lanny's hand.

"Very nice. Very nice." Lanny nodded.

John introduced Lanny to the front desk staff and Lanny particularly noted how eagerly they smiled at him. John watched the staff interact with Lanny as they exchanged pleasantries and how they asked Lanny about his needs today.

"Thank you, but I'm just here to see the club," Lanny said, impressed with courteous inquiries.

"Come on, I'll show you around," John said as he guided Lanny passed the front desk.

"Nice people you have here, John," Lanny said.

"Yeah, they're getting better. The owner is letting me do some general manager stuff like hiring the front desk staff and training them. I'm trying to instill in them a real customer service ethic, you know, like the kind you find in LA at a nice racquet club. I don't think it's right to charge LA prices and give people Santa Fe service. Know what I mean?"

Remembering his encounters with the service style around town, Lanny nodded his head. "Yes, I do."

John showed Lanny the club's state-of-the-art fitness room. The room looked packed with members milling about the weight machines, going from one routine to another, stretching and lifting with grimaces on their faces. Music blared out a rocky beat from overhead speakers. Some members, it seemed to Lanny, went about their exercise as if they were cleaning their garages, while others seemed to be in their element. Mirrors lined three sides of the room and a large glass paneled window looked out over the piñon forest, so those using the treadmill could look up to the mountains that loomed just above the club.

As Lanny passed through the room, he could pick up bits of conversation:

"...well I'm just discouraged, that's all. I work out but I'm still fat."

"...Man, if I could only cut out the beer and the green chile cheese burgers, I bet I could..."

"...I'm sure it's my genes."

"...Don't you get it? You can't eat what you want, fat boy."

"...easy for you to say. You're just naturally slim. I hate you."

"... only exercise once a week. I don't want to overdo it. I have enough stress in my life."

"...that guy?"

"...Yeah, I bet he..."

"...saw her with another man at the Palace last night."

"...her boobs are as fake as my jewelry."

"...sometimes I hate my body. I'll never have a flat stomach and a round ass. Never. I just don't know what the hell I'm doing..."

"...So? Whatever it is, get over it. Being fat is a choice."

"...simple: I choose not to eat."

"...working out is all that matters."

"...just workin' on my six-pack."

"...Yeah, well I got a case here, see?"

"...doesn't matter. I'm fit. I exercise like a dog. I look good but I haven't had a date in six months."

"...push it, bro. Get big."

"...maybe you do, but I hate working out. It sucks."

John and Lanny passed the indoor pool. It was a school holiday so the pool was full of kids. Seeing all the kids splashing around and having fun, Lanny thought to himself that there was probably a lot of piss in that pool, remembering those few times as a kid: the excitement, the cool feeling beneath his budding testicles, and being surrounded by the anonymity of the water.

John pushed open the doors that led out to the tennis courts.

Lanny took in the beautiful surroundings, noticing how the courts were laid out in three tiers. Something started to stir in the pit of his stomach.

A vague anxiety? Lanny wondered to himself.

Snow from last night's storm covered the courts but the sun was starting to melt away the snow. Lanny could see his breath but the sun felt very hot on his face.

"Can't play out here today but maybe tomorrow," John said. "Sometimes you can play outside throughout the winter. If it's thirty-five degrees and the sun is out and there is no wind, the conditions are fairly comfortable. As you can see we've got nine hard courts. Come on, let's head down to the indoor courts."

John started to head down the shoveled pathway but stopped because he noticed that Lanny was not following him. Lanny stood, taking a long look around at the courts and the surrounding snow-frosted piñon trees and up at the snow-capped mountains.

How immediately beautiful everything is, Lanny thought. All those years of living in a sprawling, metastasizing urban metropolis with its gray miasma of concrete streets, monotonous buildings and eye-numbing telephone poles framing his every view. Looking for natural beauty had required a very determined eye. *Here, nature has not been subdued and covered over by ugly development. No, here nature stands out boldly, so alluring and....innocent.* Lanny wondered why he had thought of that word but it had come to him unambiguously. He would have to give that some more thought and Lanny realized also that the abundant natural beauty around him had started to awaken his senses; senses that had been dulled and stunted by too many days adrift in asphalt parking lots, corridors of commercial strip malls, and gaudy neon that could penetrate the darkest of bedrooms.

"It's beautiful here, isn't it," John finally said. "Great setting for a tennis club. You know," John started with awe and reverence in his voice, "you can be down match point to somebody whose ass you want to kick so bad you can taste it, and then look around at the beautiful surroundings and suddenly...poof!"—John flailed his arms out in a dramatic flourish—"you don't care anymore."

Caught up by the moment Lanny started to nod his head and then noticed John had a twinkle in his eye and a smirk on his face. Lanny quickly changed his knowing smile to a harsh frown.

"Yeah, bullshit!" Lanny blurted out.

"That's right, bullshit!" and John laughed. "I had you going there for a moment didn't I?"

"I should have known better, coming from you. You'd beat your mother 0 and 0 on her fiftieth birthday."

"Actually it was 0 and 1. I let her have a game." John laughed heartily. "Come on let's check out the indoor courts."

Still chuckling, John slapped Lanny on the back and led him down the path to the indoor facility that Lanny could see was tucked in between two rolling hills thick with piñon clusters.

"Man, this is one big adobe building."

"Looks like it, doesn't it?" And John explained that the building had a faux-adobe front with real adobe support walls that flared out to the side hiding from view the rest of the metal building.

John punched in the combination at the entrance and as he opened the door Lanny heard the unmistakable pop of a tennis ball rocketing off a racquet head. Involuntarily, his head lifted as if to heed an old familiar call and again something stirred in his stomach. He felt the sound reverberate deep within him, and for a brief moment his body flushed with the feel of hitting a ball right in the sweet spot: that pure, solid feeling of being connected when the ball, the body, and the mind were one. The memory passed through his body like a tremor and he shook it off.

"Had a shiver. Cold, eh?" John noted.

"I guess you could say that."

John grinned. "You're not used to the weather here yet, beach boy. There'll be no jogging in the sand for you."

"Good," Lanny grinned back. "I hated that."

Entering the building, Lanny and John made their way onto the Player's Porch, a platform with tables, chairs, and a small three-row grandstand. From the elevated Player's Porch Lanny could see all three courts, one court laid out in front and two courts on either side. All of the courts had green backdrops. The walls and ceiling were draped in white. The Indirect lighting, Lanny noted, spread a very consistent diffusion of light over the courts, he couldn't see any dark spots or "blind spots." The shouts of the players, the sounds of the ball popping off racquets, and the squeaks from their tennis shoes filled the building. These sounds began to awaken old instincts quieted by the passing years, yet waiting, like an old fuse to be lit. Lanny could feel himself becoming more alert. A nervous energy made him shuffle his feet as he stood looking out over the courts.

John looked at Lanny's profile and could sense that he was looking inward and that being back in a tennis environment had provoked some old feelings. He saw Lanny's feet shift nervously and thought: *Boy, he is as jumpy as an old racehorse revisiting the track where he kicked everybody's ass.*

On the court to Lanny's right a couple of 4.5 players caught his eye. They were deep in a rally: forehand-to-forehand. The younger player with the bushy walrus mustache had long loopy strokes, strokes, Lanny figured, that had been developed on the slow clay. He grunted with the effort of his full, windmill strokes, while his older opponent, whose bald head glistened with perspiration, had a simple, flat, take-back of the racquet and then pushed smoothly out through the contact.

That bald dude is an old-time hard-court player, Lanny thought.

Eight strokes into the rally the younger player hit a big 'looper' deep into the corner pulling his opponent off the court. The older player, showing surprising quickness, ran the ball down and shoved the ball back—*oops,* Lanny thought, *missed an opportunity there. I bet he'll regret it.*

The younger player had stayed back and allowed his opponent to essentially restart the point. Seemingly strengthened by his resiliency, the older player got a hold of the point, hurt his opponent with a sharp crosscourt ball, saw that his opponent was really digging to reach the ball, came in, and took his opponent's floater out of the air and volleyed to the open court: point over.

The younger player's mustache bristled fiercely as he blew out his lips and bounced his racquet. Lanny smiled knowingly.

"Tough point for Wally," John said.

Lanny kept smiling when he heard the player's name and thought about his mustache. "It shouldn't have been. He should have won the point. He missed his opportunity."

John thought for a moment. "Yea, you're right, he sure did." And John looked at Lanny with a bit of surprise. "Boy, you were quick to pick up on that."

Again Lanny shuffled his feet. "Hey, I might not hunt anymore but I sure as hell remember how you're supposed to do it. When your opponent is hurt you have to go in for the kill."

John laughed. "Yep. I should remember. You did it to me enough times."

Lanny nodded, his voice gaining an old conviction. "Yeah, well, being at net, that's where the action is, the real *mano a mano* of tennis. I mean, would you rather watch a match between Connors and McEnroe, or Guillermo Vilas and Harold Salomon? Why watch a match where both guys are just waiting for the other guy to miss? The only compelling point is where you *make* a guy miss or *make* him come up with a shot." Lanny turned to look out over the courts as if gazing over a battlefield. "Tennis is about pressure: who's applying it and who has to deal with it. And it shapes you whether you resist it or not. Just like the pressures of life, eh, John? "

"If you say so, professor," John mocked.

Lanny nodded. "And whether you're applying pressure or dealing with it, no point is ever conceded; you can never betray yourself, no matter what the score."

For the first time in many years, Lanny could clearly hear his father's words; those words that had so stung him as a kid. Lanny finished his matter-of-fact statement and without being able to help it, he shuffled his feet again.

John flashed his big-toothed grin. "Dude, I don't care how long it's been, or the fact that you say you don't play anymore. You're still intense about the game. Don't fool yourself."

Have I been fooling myself all these years? No, that can't be. Tennis had... Lanny ran his fingers through his hair and scratched the back of his head as if trying to coax a little clarity from himself. *Tennis had just come to an end for me. That's all.*

Lanny's features let go of their momentary sharpness and he was forced to acknowledge something he never had.

"Well, my old man and the Professor trained and taught that there was only one way to play: with respect, with truth—yes, truth, my truth; that tennis was essentially a fight; that it was beyond the concepts of just playing, having fun, or doing your best; it was—" and Lanny turned to look at John with discovery on his face—"it was—and I shit you not—it was a way of being."

John absorbed what Lanny had to say for a moment and then squinted his eyes at him. "Dude, that's deep, too deep for me. You were always a serious little shit on the court."

Lanny shrugged. "It's not deep. That's just the way it was."

"What about just hit the ball hard and the hell with the rest?" John replied in a statement more than a question, a grin back on his square-jawed face.

Lanny rolled his lip in and then out. "Let me tell you what the Professor would say to that: Anybody can hit the ball hard, but it's harder to hit the ball with respect, without an ego. Respect means that you play a mindful game of tennis, not"—and Lanny turned to look at a still grinning John—"a mindless one."

"Oh, so you think I had a mindless game?" John accused.

Lanny didn't answer for a moment but just looked at John with an expression that said: I'm sorry but that's the truth.

"So you think—"

"How many forehands did you slap into the fence when you tried to pass me?" Lanny cut in.

John had to think for a moment.

"A lot, right?" Lanny helped him.

"Yeah, you're right. A lot," admitted John.

Again Lanny looked out over the courts, his feet shifted again. "You always wanted to take things into your own hands to win or lose the point: that's ego, not respect. You never understood your ability. You just played, you didn't examine, you didn't learn. The Professor always told me"—and Lanny turned to look back at John who was now listening carefully, his jaunty grin gone— "tennis is not about playing, it's about learning."

"Hey, I learned how to play, how to hit the ball, how to play competitively. That's what tennis is all about," John replied, defending himself.

Lanny smiled, remembering how he had used those same words with the Professor.

"Exactly. You learned how to play but what did you learn about yourself?"

"Oh, man, what did I learn?" John almost laughed. "I learned that I won or I lost. That's the bottom line. Now I know that you've got your master's degree and you've been teaching all that literature and that philosophical mumbo-jumbo. So, you think tennis is like a philosophy class. Well it ain't."

Lanny now knew what the stirring in his stomach was: a welling up of a dormant knowledge and understanding. All those intense drilling hours on the court with his father, the countless tournaments, the wins and losses, and all those "lessons" with the Professor where they didn't hit one ball but just talked. The Professor would tell him, with a fervor in his eyes, just how deep and multi-layered tennis was and how it was the perfect metaphor for life. Tennis, he would say, was the ultimate teacher, that the lessons of the tennis court are the lessons of life, and he insisted, the one overriding task that life and tennis demand is: master yourself. Lanny remembered that much of what the Professor had said he didn't understand and he would come home puzzled. Often, in the middle of their talk Lanny would ask why don't they just hit some balls and the Professor would reply that they were. And now all of what the Professor had said began to unfold within him with the clarity of an epiphany.

John pulled Lanny out of his reverie. "Hey, Socrates, like I said, tennis is not a philosophy class."

Lanny nodded knowingly. "I was like you once."

"No shit," John mocked.

"Yeah, I was. And I know it's hard to understand that tennis is not just a game to be played but that it is so much more. And speaking of Socrates you remember what he said, don't you?"

"Unfortunately, I have a feeling you are going to tell me."

Lanny put on his best lecturing voice. "He said, my unenlightened friend, that the unexamined life is not worth living, and that the unexamined tennis game is not worth playing."

John laughed and blew his lips together derisively. "Man, is that what you spent all that money on your education for? I say life is short: hit the ball hard."

"You would say that, wouldn't you?"

Lanny noticed a woman on the far court waving her arms.

"Who is that lady waving her arms?" Lanny asked.

John looked over to court three and he smacked his hand to his forehead.

"Jesus Christ, that's Mrs. Harper. I forgot about the half hour lesson I had with her."

John waved back at her and shouted, "I'm coming right now." He turned back to Lanny. "She always just takes half hour lessons to work on her serve. We never get anything accomplished but she talks a lot."

"Can she serve?" Lanny asked.

John looked over at Lanny, looked around to see if anyone was too close by, and smirked. "God couldn't teach her how to serve. Hey, can you hang out for a half hour? When I finish we'll get some lunch."

Lanny shrugged. "Yeah, I don't have anything to do. I'll just watch you destroy that woman's serve."

"There's nothing to destroy," John quipped in a low voice. "See you in a bit."

We've heard it all: the mental game, the inner game, the strategy game, the ugly game, the power game, blah, blah, blah...The real reality of tennis is that tennis is played from the waist down. The feet are the sine qua non of tennis. Your heart, your mind, your belief, your competitive will—all of which should be in your feet. The feet are the nexus of tennis. Think with your feet; see with your feet, feel with your feet, fight with your feet. Ultimately, you don't win with your strokes. You win with your feet.
—Lanny Bedford, "The Long Hard Court"

"Oh, John, that's bullshit. You always had a coconut for a head," Lanny said and he gulped back a swallow of Chardonnay.

John noted that Lanny had carefully sipped his first glass. He had an idea.

The control might be slipping away. I'm getting close. I'll keep goading him.

Since Lanny arrived in Santa Fe, John had been trying to figure out how to get to Lanny, to make him open up.

John could see that Lanny was clearly depressed. He certainly wasn't like John had remembered him: intense on the court but friendly, able to laugh and wisecrack, a faint smile on his face while he cut you up with his serve and volley game. Even for a junior, he had an amazing composure that belied his years. By his demeanor you always thought he was ahead, and John had never seen Lanny hit a desperate shot. John remembered that once, in between matches at a junior event in Los Angeles, he and Lanny were eating lunch. John was still flush with his earlier victory where he had come up with five or six desperation shots that proved to be the shots that won the match for him.

"Hey, Lan," John had beamed. "Thanks for watchin' my match. Did you see those shots I hit to win it?" John asked, as he bit into his sandwich.

Lanny nodded his head thoughtfully.

"Man, there's nothing like hitting a few desperation shots to win a match, huh, Lan?" And John flashed his big-toothed grin.

And John remembered how Lanny smiled that kid's smile of his and said in his adolescent wise-man tenor:

"Yeah, Meat, I saw 'em," Lanny said, using John's nickname. John used to whip out hamburger paddies and eat them during the changeovers. "But you know what? I would rather lose the match than think I have to hit those kinds of shots. I don't like the feeling. Who wants to lose control like that? I'd rather lose."

John just shook his head while pieces of potato chips dropped out of his mouth as he chomped away. "Man, like always, I don't know what the heck you just said but you're missing all the excitement and all the parents goin' crazy; stuff like that."

"Too much excitement for me," Lanny replied while peeling his banana...

John and Lanny had walked the four blocks from the club to Harry's Roadhouse, a restaurant that reminded Lanny of a place in

Topanga Canyon, just north of Santa Monica, but the name of the restaurant didn't come to him. Again, Lanny marveled at the sky that seemed as deep and wide as any imagination and those clouds, the whiteness of them hurt his eyes. The brisk, cold air filled him with a clean vitality he hadn't felt before.

"So, I might have had a coconut for a head but I was good. Hey, who was the fastest? John demanded.

"You."

"Who was the hardest hitting junior?"

"You."

"Who was the kid nobody wanted in the first round, or any round for that matter?"

"You."

John nodded his square jaw. "You're damned right. I was scary. The next Connors."

"You did copy that grunt of his didn't you?"

"Hell yes. Those damn kids didn't know what hit 'em. I didn't like to give anybody another ball. I would just grunt and hit it right by 'em." John flashed a toothy grin. "All the parents would give me dirty looks as if I was a bully or something. Ha!"

Lanny put his wineglass down and wiped his mouth with a napkin because he had left too much wine on his upper lip. He remembered how John was much more stocky and muscular than the other kids and how some parents said he was lying about his age.

"Well, I thought you were funny."

"Lan, you were the only one," John retorted.

"You would grunt and I would watch that ball sail past me and hit the fence on the fly. You know what your problem was, Meat?"

John laughed at the old reference.

"Meat. Nobody's called me that in twenty some years. But hey, I didn't have a problem. I kicked everybody's ass but yours. I—"

Lanny broke in, insistent.

"-Meat, you know what your problem with me was?"

"You were just better than me."

"Besides that." Lanny poured another glass and looked at John as if he was going to let out a secret. "You never let me give *you* another ball. Look, the most profound tenet in—"

John squirmed in his chair and cut Lanny off, raising his hands in irritation.

"What? Are we back in the philosophy classroom again? What the hell does 'tenet' mean anyway? Even as a little kid I didn't know what the hell you were talking about sometimes. Jeez, Lan, I've never heard so many slippery words in my life," John chided. "Tenet? If you mean tenant, well, hell, I'm a tenant and it costs me thirteen hundred a month."

"Very funny. As I was saying: the most profound principal in tennis is that there is always *another* ball; another chance; the chance to start over; the constant chance to keep competing. You didn't want to compete with me."

Lanny swirled the wine around in his glass and stroked his goatee, his eyes beginning to reflect an awakening deep within him.

Good. John thought to himself. *I've got him going.*

"That's part of what makes tennis a great process—note, I didn't say a great game—because over the course of a match the next ball is almost always more important than the last ball. The Professor told me to think of tennis as a process not a game."

"Oh, boy, more mumbo-jumbo," John chimed in.

Lanny ploughed on. "A game begins and ends but a process is a continuum, a constant continuing of moment after moment without a *beginning* or an *end*, which just traps you into a very limited, small-minded, result-oriented way of thinking: you win you lose. That's the biggest myth in tennis. When you're deep in the process, moment after moment for two hours, there is nothing in the world more life-affirming than that." Lanny tossed back another swig, and in his mind he could hear Professor Burns echoing his words, words that were now his.

"Man, you were married too long. What do you think sex is for?" John replied drolly.

"Sex is ephemeral. Tennis is not," Lanny shot back.

John rolled his eyes. "Boy, what a clever word. I always thought you were too clever for tennis."

John dipped four French fries into a pool of ketchup. "Sure, another ball. Yeah, well you're not going to get another ball when somebody smokes a winner past you for the match. The next ball you get is the one you smack up and out of the court because you're pissed off."

"If you want to miss my point, go ahead," Lanny said serenely.

I've got to get him now. Time for the head butt, John decided.

"Yeah, well all of that being in the moment stuff, thinking that tennis is just a process, looking forward to the next ball, the learning about yourself, playing with respect, tennis as a way of being—blah, blah." *I've got to give it to him now,* John thought. "None of that matters if you choke."

Lanny stopped raising his glass to take a drink. Stunned, he set his glass down. He knew exactly what John was referring to and his mind raced back to that moment and again he felt his hand tighten and the pain begin to well up within him and he swallowed hard trying to keep it all down. He could feel his forehead getting ready to break a sweat as if he were back under that boiling sun twenty-two years ago. He felt his hands grip the sides of the table. He tried to keep his lips from forming a tight grimace. He didn't want John to see what he was feeling and struggling to control.

Lanny cut off his exhalation half way through. "Oh, you're talking about the volley I—"

I've got to stay on top of him, John said to himself.

"—That volley," John corrected. "You know everybody talked about *that volley* and always referred to it as *that volley*.

Lanny scratched his head as if trying to erase an errant thought and shrugged his shoulders.

"I didn't choke. I just missed the volley." Lanny heard himself mouth the casual words but he meant to say something different. The words had just come out as if said by somebody else.

"Just missed?" John asked as he arched an eyebrow, remembering *that volley* because he had been in the stands that day and saw Lanny so uncharacteristically club the volley three feet out. John, like everybody else had seen Lanny volleying crisply all match long and deftly when he needed to—showing why he had the best serve-and-volley in the juniors and why many had put him in the same category as McEnroe. John could still hear the groan of disappointment from the crowd as Lanny unbelievably missed that simple sitter volley. Every hacker in the crowd, John could see, was shaking their heads thinking that even they could have made that volley. And John could see that Lanny had taken the miss like a body blow and John knew in his tennis-playing heart that that was it: Lanny was done.

John let the silence go on, to let Lanny stew in the moment and in his reflections, to hopefully trigger something within him.

I just missed the volley, Lanny quickly thought to himself. That was how he thought about *that* volley. He must have made over a hundred volleys that day. But John's pointed skepticism had jarred him, but come on! He had been under the grueling sun for three hours. There was fatigue. *All I did was miss a damn volley. That's it.* He knew now that his career had been over before he

51

missed that volley. *Tennis wasn't fun anymore. I couldn't stay in the moment. There were too many voices…*

He felt the old tides of emotion from that day rise up out of a long dormant, forgotten sea within him—tides of pain. *Had it been that intense?* As his chest rose and fell with a long sigh, he tried to come to grips with just how much pain he had felt that day and the effort it had taken to bury that pain deep under the mud of his life.

John could see that Lanny was struggling to compose himself as he fidgeted with his napkin, his eyes alternately focusing inward and outward.

"Hey, man," John soothed. "You're right, you just missed it and that's that. No need to rehash it. I mean, who cares? It was a long time ago and you don't even play tennis anymore anyway. I'm sorry I brought it up."

Lanny let a moment of panic pass through him. He reasserted himself with another indifferent shrug of his shoulders as if dismissing what had just been said. He calmly took a sip off his wineglass. And John could see a look forming in Lanny's eyes that he hadn't seen since Lanny looked over the net at him before saying: "Hey, good luck." And John remembered that after about six matches he started to quip at Lanny: "Yeah, fuck you."

"You got a ball machine?" Lanny asked flatly.

John's eyes widened for a moment. "Yeah, sure do."

"Let's go. You got a racket for me? An old wooden racquet?"

John thought for a moment absorbing the request. "I think I've got one of my old wood frames in the garage. We can stop by my—"

"No, that's all right." Lanny stood up.

John didn't move. He arched a skeptical eyebrow and looked up at Lanny. "Are you sure?"

"Any racquet will do…Come on. What? Can't a guy want to hit a few balls? Last time I hit was with a wood racket. I don't think those new graphite ones can give you the same feel. And you know, feel is everything."

The mind's eye has been called the third eye, the karmic eye, the prescient eye, the psychic eye, and the eye of the soul... What an elusive concept. But I tell you, the mind's eye is really how we "see" in tennis. The crucial thing to understand about tennis at any level is that tennis is a contact sport, not an aiming sport. One can't watch the ball while simultaneously trying to look to aim the ball. Picture the court with your mind's eye, seeing with your mind the spot on the court where you wish the ball to go. Meanwhile your eyes are free to watch the contact between the ball and the racquet happen. So, watch the ball with your eyes and aim with your mind's eye.

—At the Public Courts: Conversations with the Professor, alias "The Pusher"

How long can he keep this up? What is he trying to do? John wondered to himself. He sat on the Player's Porch, chin cupped in his hands, as he watched Lanny hit against the ball machine. One of John's juniors picked up balls and kept the machine full as Lanny had requested. John could see Lanny's face set with grim determination. Closing his eyes he could hear the rhythmic tap dance of tennis: shuffle-shuffle-step, split-step-cross-step, split-step-tiny-tiny-tiny-step-big step, split-step, cross-step, split-step, cross step…And John knew without looking that the result of that footwork would be a smooth groundstroke and a compact volley, a sureness and fluidity of motion that reflected a body's deep understanding of technique and effortless instinct.

John opened his eyes and watched for a while. *That Bedford trademark of effortlessness is still there, but ah, the timing,* he noted while Lanny caught the tape with a few balls, hit one late, and hit a couple long—*you can't just resurrect that after twenty years. But man, that technique is beautiful to watch.* John couldn't help but admire how Lanny's strokes unfolded so purely that he thought every ball Lanny was about to hit would go in and was surprised when it didn't.

Yeah, when we were juniors I remember thinking that.

John looked at his watch. Lanny had been at it for over an hour, pausing only briefly to drink. Sweat dripped off his forehead, his shirt was drenched and John could hear Lanny's labored breathing. And he hadn't changed his expression the whole time, that sniper's stare that looked both outward and inward. He thought Lanny was going to stop but he'd thought that twenty minutes ago.

What is he doing?

Lanny paused for a second to wipe his hand on his shirt and John could see a smudge of blood.

Ah, blisters! He doesn't have his tennis calluses anymore. That's it. He's done now.

Lanny could feel his heart pounding in his chest like it wanted to break free and fly away. He wanted to stop. Oh, how he wanted to stop, but a voice in him kept saying: *Not yet. You haven't hit it. You can stop when you hit it. You haven't hit it.*

The flushed feeling of pleasure Lanny felt when he began had worn off but he still tingled with the feeling of doing something so natural to him. When he first gripped the racquet, he was anxious that he might be indifferent or worse that it would feel alien and that he wouldn't be able to take one swing. But when he finally gripped the racquet it came alive like an organic extension of his arm.

His mind went blank and he just started stroking and something in the back of his consciousness fastened on to the weight of the racquet head. And he knew right away that this graphite racquet was too light, too stiff, and too powerful. It made his arm want to go too quickly and it took thirty or forty balls before he could adjust.

Whoomp… Whoomp…The balls kept coming and Lanny felt his legs getting heavy and his footwork began to breakdown under the barrage of balls. His muscles quivered on the brink of fatigue and he could feel his lower back ready to go into spasm. His breath now came in gasps and grunts as he shuffled on the baseline and he could feel his feet getting away from him. He felt something warm under his grip and felt his hand slip as he made contact. He quickly wiped the blood on his shirt. Every time he made contact his bloody blisters screamed in his hand and stinging pain shot up his arm. Something deep within his heart made him take grim satisfaction from the pain.

God, the air up here is so thin, there's nothing to breathe. I can't get enough air. Not yet! he shouted to himself. *I haven't hit it.*

The intense pain began to open a door in the back of his mind.

"Don't force your footwork," a voice said. "Don't muscle it. Keep a rhythm. Dance," the professor's deep voice intoned. "That's it...No, no, not so many steps, not so busy. That's it. Trust your rhythm. Dance. That's it. Now, float right through your fatigue."

Why is he in my head right now? After all these years...

"Keep your arm and your body connected, don't let the arm fly off by itself," he could hear the Professor saying to him. "It all turns together and finishes together. Keep it connected. The stroke is not a puzzle, it is all one piece."

A group of guys had gathered behind John. They were getting ready to go onto the opposite court but had stopped to watch Lanny. They were marveling at the way Lanny didn't miss a ball, the way he changed spins from slice to top spin and how be moved the ball around.

"Man, that guy is too smooth," observed Carl Holmes, who stood directly behind John. "He doesn't miss a ball. He must have played on the professional tour or something," John turned his head around and looked up at Carl with a smirk on his face.

"Carl, would you believe that guy hasn't picked up a racquet in over twenty years and the last time he hit was with a wood racquet?

"No ... you're kidding?" Carl replied awe in his voice. "So, he was a pro, wasn't he?"

John took a few moments and watched Lanny hit a few more balls and noticed how the ball machine and Lanny seemed like one machine, working together like a well-oiled piston.

"No, he never played on the tour, but he sure could've. We grew up together in the juniors." Again he turned around and looked at the guys behind him. "He was probably," and John corrected himself with conviction, "no, he *was* the best junior tennis player in the states to ever pick up a racquet. "

"Do you say that just because he always kicked your ass or something?" snorted Jason Rockington, the good-natured clown of the group. He and John were always needling one another.

"Got that right, Rocky," John nodded. "He sure did. And he beat everybody else, too. I wasn't the only one to have my ass handed to me. I was in good company."

"So, what happened to him?" Carl asked.

John took a breath. "I really don't know. I guess he was always better than he thought he was. Who knows? It's a mystery to me. God, he had it all."

"You know," Jason chimed in, "I think I'm the same way. I'm better than I think I am."

"No you're not," Carl said flatly.

"That'll be the day," John retorted. "We all know you think you should play with the 4.0 guys and everybody knows that's a crock."

"Well, maybe, but I know I could play 3.5," Jason shrugged, wilting under the disbelieving stares of the guys gathered around him.

"Dream on, pal," Carl said as he elbowed Jason in the ribs.

"Why is that guy bloody?" Paul Bodin's Cajun accent asked.

Again silence settled on the crowd as they watched Lanny.

What the hell is he trying to prove? John asked himself as he noticed that Lanny's shirt had blood on it and that his racquet handle was bloody. Lanny gasped with effort and was pouring sweat in the dry Santa Fe air. *He's not just hitting a few balls. He's doing something else. He's going to hurt himself.*

John got out of his chair and began to motion to the young kid feeding the ball machine to cut the power and as he raise his hand and started to shout out the order, Lanny collapsed into an abrupt heap and his racquet went sliding across the court.

John grabbed a water bottle and sprinted over to Lanny with the rest of the guys following close on his heels. Lanny lay, eyes closed, chest heaving and grimacing with pain.

"Hey man, are you all right?" John asked as he bent over Lanny. The men had gathered around in a circle and peered down wondering what they should do. Should someone go for a doctor?

"I'm cramping," Lanny managed to say between clenched teeth.

"Here, drink this." John put a hand behind Lanny's head, lifted it, and put the bottle between Lanny's lips.

"Come on, drink it. You're about as dehydrated as a dried chile. Come on. That's it. Drink."

"I think I'm going to pass out," Lanny whispered.

John's eyes widened with concern. "No you're not." And John poured the rest of the bottle on Lanny's face and chest.

"Wait! Don't pour—".

Too late. Carmen Villafuerte pushed her way through the group of men surrounding Lanny. She was a tall, striking woman with liquid brown/black eyes. As she bent down over Lanny her thick, black hair cascaded down past her face and fell across Lanny's chest. She could see that he was fighting for consciousness. The cold water shocked Lanny and further loosened his grip on his consciousness. His eyes almost rolled back.

"Boy, John, that really helped him," Jason snorted.

One of the men had called up to the front desk when Lanny collapsed, and the front desk sent Carmen down to the indoor courts. She was one of the fitness trainers and the only one on staff who had some medical training.

"What happened?" Carmen asked quickly in a clipped voice as she took Lanny's pulse.

"He seemed to just suddenly collapse," John replied. "Right, guys?"

All the men nodded and confirmed what John had said.

"I've seen guys drop like that," Jason intoned, assuming the whole world was listening to him. "But that was in 'Nam. People drop that quick when they get shot."

"What the hell do you know about that, Jason?" Paul Bodin's slow cadence asked dryly. "I heard you never got off the damn supply boat. Ain't that right, Skipper?"

Carl Holmes nodded. "Big Jason was stuck in supply. He never got hot or close to being hot."

"From the deck, I saw a lot, I mean a lot," Jason shot back, while the rest of the guys laughed.

"Someone give me a towel," Carmen ordered.

One of the men reached into his tennis bag and brought out a towel and gave it to Carmen. As she lifted Lanny's head to rest it on the towel beneath, Lanny's eyes started to open. Still slightly dizzy, Lanny began to make out the face above him. He blinked a couple of times to see if the angelic face above him would disappear. Carmen's foamy black hair dangled over him and as she pulled her hair back it brushed over his face and the smell of her hair went right to his senses like a singular message of life and sensuality and it cascaded over his fatigue like an elixir. He tried to name the feeling but couldn't. He tried to name the smell but couldn't. He felt disoriented and tried to shake his head as if to get a grip on what was happening.

"Easy," Carmen's voice purred and she held his head still. She mopped his forehead, noting Lanny's masculine features: prominent cheekbones, straight nose, strong jaw, the smooth but determined mouth, and blue eyes, that at a glance seemed piercing, but when she looked into them deeply, the blue depth of them made her think of the broad sky above Santa Fe.

"Easy, now. Just lay there, no sudden movements. Do you feel like you are going to get suddenly ill?"

Lanny fought back a strange urge to smile broadly and shake his head no as if to say: how could you ask that? But he could feel he was still struggling for his breath and wondered how the air could be so thin. As he shook his head 'no' at Carmen's question, his eyes locked onto hers.

Something kept her from avoiding his eyes. *Why?* She wondered to herself then quickly looked Lanny over. She wanted to be on the safe side and said she thought he ought to go to the hospital.

"No ... that's all right," Lanny managed to whisper.

"What happened?" John asked. "Why did you stop? Finally had enough, eh?"

"No," Lanny sputtered back. "Not that."

"Then why?"

"You wouldn't understand if I told you."

John's eyes narrowed. "Oh, more mumbo-jumbo, eh?"

Lanny's chest still heaved up and down as he fought to get his breath back.

"So?" John asked insistent.

"I hit the perfect ball," Lanny replied in a breathless voice that John barely heard.

A look of incredulity swept over John's face and he rolled his eyes.

"What the hell did you say?"

Lanny managed to sit up. "I...I wasn't going to stop...until I hit the perfect ball and finally... I hit it."

"Man," John sighed, "I didn't understand you when we were kids and I still don't. You're crazy as hell."

The men that were gathered around just looked at each other to confirm if they heard what Lanny had really said. They all shook their heads in amazement, and Carmen just peered down at Lanny, trying to size him up, thinking about his bizarre answer and wondering why she wanted to cradle his head in her arms again.

Great tennis demands clarity. You can no more live your life well without clarity than you can play tennis well without clarity. It's simple really: live your life with conviction and hit the ball with conviction.

—At The Public Courts: Conversations with the Professor, alias "The Pusher."

Lanny was glad that he was headed down the Atalaya hiking trail. He had pushed it hard going up. He felt he was finally acclimating himself to being seven thousand feet above sea level. In the fading light, he picked his way carefully along the lumpy, well-worn trail. He cupped his chilled hands and blew on them, and as he rubbed them together he felt the sting of the still healing blisters on his right hand. The pain made his hand feel alive as if it was awakening after a long dull hibernation.

It wants to grip the racquet, he thought as he jumped over a small boulder. A slight smile of understanding pulled at the sides of his mouth. He realized then that he had always thought of his hand as being more than just a part of him. It had its own... (the slight smile again)...it had its own consciousness. *That's it. Yes.* And now that he thought about it in more depth, he remembered those matches when it felt like he could slow down time to a sort of timeless feeling where he almost felt out of his body, his mind quiet, while his hand told the ball what to do, (or sensed what to do and felt like some kind of hypersensitive antennae.)

The season had fallen deep into December, speeding the approach of winter. As the days weakened, the sun would drop quickly into a blaze of sunset. Lanny stopped for a moment on a slight switch back that had a vantage point and looked out where he could see the struggle between day and night, a struggle that had never occurred to him back in LA where the enormity of the city and it's omnipotent glare of lights and endless crisscross of streets snuffed out all that was natural.

The sunset flashed the full color spectrum of reds, oranges, and yellows across the sky and outlined the clouds with glowing lines of bright, electric light. Sixty miles to the south, across the rolling high desert plain, dotted with green clumps of trees, Lanny could see the Sandia Mountains towering over Albuquerque like a long arched sentinel. As the light filtered through the coming dusk and silence gathered in the arroyos, the Sangre de Cristo Mountains took on a purplish-red hue, their snow-tipped peaks sparkled against the advancing darkness of night. Any hint of the day's warmth vanished into the ether. The wind picked up and its cold crispness brought the smell of snow.

Lanny watched as the shadows cast by the setting sun galloped across the piñon forest that stretched out before him and then, they moved slowly, like the tide of a dark ocean, up the front side of the mountains like God was drawing a drape across the sky—a sight as powerful as anything he had ever seen. He almost chided himself in the simple realization that the forces he had just witnessed were...alive and eternal, and that is the only explanation for them.

Having never been confronted by nature, Lanny felt the loss of not experiencing enough of the awe that nature can inspire. Something in his...humanity felt diminished. And that made him think of another aspect of his life that had diminished.

Everything I see before me is just teeming with the profound force of life and the rhythm of eternity, reveling in its design and purpose... And me? What the hell is my purpose? My design?

He squeezed his right hand together until the pain from his unhealed blisters gave him a grim satisfaction.

There is always a road to take on the court but don't follow it to the end, because every road you follow to the end leads nowhere. Always look for the other road, the next turn off, the next point, the next ball. Be willing to change the road you're on.
—Lanny Bedford, "The Long Hard Court"

Carmen always liked to finish her day off with some stretches, while thinking back on whom she had trained that day and making some mental notes about each particular client. To an observer, her stretching poses looked like some languid dance, her long limbs moving like a stationary octopus. Her smooth, ivory skin clearly outlined her toned muscles. Her thick, glossy black hair seemed to flow around her shoulders. Her oval-shaped face and generous mouth radiated health, vitality, and a sensuality that seemed open and reserved at the same time. She took a deep breath and exhaled through a stretch, slowly opening her large brown eyes. The mirror in front of her revealed that her eyes had hints of shiny blackness in them that seemed to attract the light and so at times her eyes seemed more black than brown.

Something made her pause and she looked at herself in the mirror. She cocked her head in a mock posture of scrutiny. *Well, let's see, girl... Such a nice butt, round and firm—better be with all the work I in put into it...Athletic long legs but the calves... yes, just a touch too muscular looking when they're flexed, and the breasts... yep, more than a bit on the small side. Damn! That's unfortunate. I blame that on my mother. Ah, the face...cute, attractive, perhaps even beautiful. I have been told that...Yes, I have been told that.*

With a wistful sigh she looked away for a moment, mulling over her personal inventory, and then a voice, the mirror's voice, made her look back. It said:

"Yeah, you're cute, but so what? You haven't had a date in six months. Whom are you waiting for?"

Not just anybody, she thought quickly while a line on her forehead tightened.

"Oh, Yeah, that's right," the mirror continued, "you're special and you'll wait for that someone who is sooooo special he doesn't exist. I think you're just taking after your Aunt Josefina; beautiful Auntie Jo who never married and lived with her parents until they died. Remember that lover she talked about, that one, the *only* one, whom she had met while she was young, and of whom she always said would return to her?"

I am not like my Auntie Jo. We're very different.

"Guess who still lives with her parents???…YOU!"

The one line on Carmen's forehead turned into a frown as she looked at the mirror. *You know my father's health is poor and my mother needs my help with him. Nobody else in the family is really free to—*

"That's because they're all married with their own families," the mirror said, cutting her off.

So?

"So?"

Carmen spread her legs almost to a full split, grabbed her ankles and slowly touched her forehead to the floor and then looked up again her eyes narrowing as if trying to see past the mirror into what lay beyond her image, into those secrets of the self that crouched just behind her awareness…like an old fear.

"You've met plenty of men," the mirror said.

"So what? So I have," Carmen whispered quickly, annoyed.

"But they aren't—"

"Aren't what?" Carmen cut in clearly agitated.

"So, what are you afraid of?"

Somewhere in her a small door abruptly opened and she could hear her heart beat. She quickly let out a derisive grunt, her lips drawing together into a smirk while she lifted up one leg high over her head.

Ha, that's a silly question. I have a great life. I love my job, my clients. I live in the house, the beautiful house of my childhood. I am surrounded by my family. I don't need a man to—

"You don't need to *trust* a man, right!?" The voice in the mirror jumped out at her with the question.

Carmen blinked slowly and all the expression left her face. She began to feel trapped. She felt her palms grow moist.

No, she reassured herself, *I don't need to trust a man.*

"Ah, that's it."

Again Carmen could hear her heart beat in the silence around her. Her breathing increased. She turned away from the mirror in front of her but another mirror confronted her.

"Ah, that's it. We agree," it said.

Men don't need to be trusted, and then a deep thought shouted within her: *THEY NEED TO BE CONTROLLED!*

"Because they are…dangerous?"

You're damn right.

"So, I am thinking about a man, a man who—"

What the hell are you talking about?

"Say his name," the mirror said quickly. "Say—"

Shut up! Carmen felt her pulse begin to race. The hair on the back of her neck began to prickle.

"Okay," the mirror's measured tone began. "I guess I could just spell his name for you: F-E-A-R."

No. That's not it.

"Okay," and the measured tone sharpened, "perhaps I could spell a much more appropriate word: S-H-A-D-O—"

—Andrew. The name came to her like the sound of a dirge. Carmen glared at the mirror, her heart now pounding in her ears. *Andrew! All right? His name was Andrew.*

"Yes," the mirror intoned with a hint of triumph. "Right, the white guy with the preppy background, Yale. All that family money. So white, so right…so Anglo that you fantasized about—

No, that's not true. I just thought that—

"And then?…." It prodded…more strongly: "And then????"

And then he hurt me.

"How did he hurt you?"

Carmen turned away from the mirror and looked down trying to calm her beating heart with some deep breaths. She suddenly felt claustrophobic and helpless, her body became strangely weak and she didn't have the strength to continue her stretching. She began to draw herself into a fetal position. The mirrored walls of the yoga room began to close in upon her. Her different reflections seemed like a pack of selves that surrounded her ready to pounce.

How can my heart beat so loudly? Why am I—

"Hello there," Lanny said as he walked through the door to the yoga room. "They told me you'd be in here; hope I'm not interrupting."

Startled, Carmen came out of her ball and rolled up to her feet. She tried to compose herself but her face still reflected the fright that had flared up within her. Sweat beaded her forehead; there was a glint of wildness in her eyes as she looked at Lanny that made him stop in his tracks.

"Whoa, are you all right?" Lanny asked, concerned. "You look ready to jump out of your leotard."

"No, no," Carmen said in a strained voice as she grabbed a hold of her poise. "I was just finishing up some strenuous," and a quick, nervous grin began at the sides of her mouth, "some strenuous, almost painful stretches and I was in…ah….deep concentration."

"Oh…I didn't know stretching could be so taxing," Lanny said and suddenly he felt the need to study her.

Carmen picked up a towel that was lying at her feet. She mopped her brow and felt her pulse slowing. Using the towel, she hoped to hide the startled blush of embarrassment that colored her neck and cheeks and the horrible feeling of vulnerability.

God, how I hate that feeling, she thought angrily to herself.

"Ah, yes, stretching can be a very vigorous workout," she said casually while she looked at him and saw that he was studying her. She really *felt* his eyes on her and she didn't like that.

"Dangerous?" the mirror asked her again.

Yes.

For a moment Lanny didn't say anything. Carmen thought he studied her in a way that made her think that somehow he *heard* the conversation she had just had with herself. She shook her head slightly to ward off those thoughts.

"Do you stretch?" she asked in a challenging tone. And not knowing quite why she said: "Most men can't last halfway through my stretch classes."

Puzzled at her tone and question, Lanny tried a smiled and managed a reply.

"I can just imagine. No, I can't say that I stretch very much. I just do a little—"

Carmen cut in, feeling more comfortable in her trainer's persona but she still spoke with an edge:

"It would make you stronger and more flexible, less prone to injury. Men *need* to have more flexibility," she said and she was surprised by the accusation in her tone.

Still puzzled, Lanny started to put on a good-natured grin but decided to respond and match the tenor of her comment.

"Do you mean flexible...flexible? Or flexible as in...real flexibility?" Lanny asked, probing with his own edge.

Carmen couldn't resist the opening. She mocked:

"Oh, you are *trying* to be intuitive."

What is she getting at? Lanny wondered to himself. *I just came in her to thank her for helping me out the other day and now I'm having this strange discussion. Man, what's her thing? Let's see.*

"I have to be perceptive when a woman like you question's my....ah, flexibility..." And Lanny quickly added: "That is, my ability to stretch."

Why am I having this conversation? The fleeting thought occurred to Carmen as she looked at Lanny who was looking at her. *He just seems so cocky and sure of himself. I don't know why it bugs me, but it does. And why does he have to lay those blue eyes on me like that? There's looking and then there's LOOKING.*

"I was just making an observation based on my profession, that's all. Men don't like to stretch," she sniffed.

Lanny noticed the wrap around mirrors captured Carmen's figure from various angles. He tried to make his inspection of her quick and unnoticeable, and he tried to keep the growing appreciation out of his eyes.

"Mirrors are very revealing, aren't they?" she asked dryly. *Let him stew a bit. No one—no man can just look at me like that.*

She caught me. Damn. That's embarrassing, Lanny quickly thought to himself and then composed an answer.

"Yes," he replied with a grin in his voice, looking around the room. "There's no escape, is there?"

"They allow you to make corrections in your stretching technique. That is if you have a technique."

Why do I feel like she's challenging me? Jeez, words within words. Her tone is kind of hostile. I can't help it if she doesn't like men. Yeah, that's it. She's one of those. All of these thoughts raced through Lanny's mind as he kept the grin on his face.

"I must confess, I am a man," Lanny said while opening the palms of his hands in a shrug but his eyes did not reflect his gesture. They flashed boldly.

"And a rude one at that," Carmen said quickly, the smile vanishing from her face.

Something made Lanny respond with total conviction: "I am sorry for that, but in another way I'm not sorry."

Now Carmen studied him, tilting her head to one side pursing her full lips together. Lanny thought this was the most sensual thing he had ever seen and quickly wondered what it would be like to taste those lips.

Isn't that just like a man? And the line on Carmen's forehead curved cynically: *A polite smile while trying to hide an impersonal erection. I know you look at me as an object. Typical.*

"My," Carmen started off with a tight smile, "aren't you full of confessions. Is there anything else you'd like to…reveal?"

"Just that I don't have much technique when it comes to stretching. That's all."

"Well," Carmen replied with her trainer's voice, "you have to start somewhere. Come to one of my classes and I'll get you started. In fact," and she looked intently into Lanny's face, smiling, her eyes narrowing with challenge, "I'll stretch you myself."

"I don't know," Lanny said as he let out some nervous air because the beauty and the subtle fierceness of her smile caught him off guard. "Ah, sounds like there would be some pain involved."

"A little," Carmen said without keeping the challenge out of her voice. "But I see that you are a big boy."

Lanny saw the flash of black light in Carmen's eyes and decided that he had never seen anything like them before and felt that he had to force himself to keep from locking onto her gaze, an exchange he knew would reveal more of his mind than hers. The thought of Carmen pulling him this way and that way while he grimaced in pain did not appeal to him at all and made the muscles in his stomach tightened with an unknown anxiety. He rolled his tongue quickly over his dry lower lip.

"You might be man enough," Carmen said, enjoying Lanny's unease and the fact that he avoided her eyes.

"I appreciate your offer," Lanny tried to say with a smooth voice, "but I think I'm flexible enough for what I do. I just came in here to thank you for helping me the other day down on the court."

"Oh, you're welcome…?"

"I'm sorry," Lanny quickly said. "I'm Lanny. All this talk of stretching and flexibility made me forget my manners. Sorry."

Why am I nervous? Lanny wondered to himself and he couldn't stop the shade of vulnerability that came over his face, which Carmen recognized.

"That's all right," Carmen replied, realizing that she was smiling at Lanny for no reason. "It happens to most men who enter the Yoga room surrounded by a bunch of mirrors, and by a bunch of women. It's not easy," she finished, the smile still on her full lips.

"God forbid," Lanny admonished, and turned to walk away.

"My offer still remains," Carmen called after him.

And something made Lanny want to have another look at a woman he knew was very beautiful and unsettling.

"I'm sorry, I didn't get your name?" Lanny asked coyly, taking time to look at her again and the mirrors' reflections of her, hoping she wouldn't catch him.

Again, 'that look' of his. While it took a moment she decided—while knowing she was forcing herself—to the conclusion that: *I don't like the way he looks at me.* And then the thought jumped into her mind: *Didn't Andrew look at me that way?*

She lowered herself to the floor to resume her stretches and tried to pull off a nonchalant wave of her hand.

"I'm Carmen."

"Well, Carmen," Lanny said as if to say something so he could still look at her, "nice to meet you."

Carmen just waved again at Lanny and forced herself not to say anything.

Now, that's a strange thing to do. The whole encounter was strange, Carmen thought to herself, as she watched Lanny turn and leave through the door. She leaned into a stretch and looked at the mirror. It didn't say a word.

Understanding tennis at the highest level is simply understanding the consequences of what you choose to do on the court.
—Lanny Bedford, "The Long Hard Court"

Wow that was strange, Lanny thought to himself as he turned and almost beat a hasty retreat out the door of the yoga room, leaving Carmen to finish her stretching. Something happened in that room but he didn't know what the hell it was.

I didn't know if she wanted to shake my hand or take a swing at me. Man…

Lanny mused over these thoughts as he dodged people who were headed for the workout room. He wondered also why he was rushing. Something started to compel him, to drive him, even as he had come to thank Carmen for her assistance the other day. He felt an odd disorientation as he pushed through the doors that led outside. He caught himself for a moment and tried to figure out what was going on.

What am I doing? Why am I here? I went for a hike…

He stopped for a moment as if waiting to hear the answer but only got back a muted silence from the cold, shadowy night that greeted him indifferently. During his hike, the unseen hand of nature in all its omnipotent permanence and stealthy harmony reached inside him like the fingers of a grasping beacon and pulled out his sense of nothing…and then slapped it down on a bald rock before him like steaming entrails to be divined for what they revealed, and he didn't like what he read among the twisted, gory hints of a dead-end life.

What is your purpose?

A frosty breeze whispered through the piñon trees saying something he couldn't make out. Clouds of his breath puffed out before him, like smoke signals that he couldn't read. The moon had just pushed up over the Sangres and like a naked eye, it looked down at him in full skepticism, it's light glistening off the white tops of the net cords. The courts before him seemed…. *abandoned. They're like ghost courts,* Lanny thought.

DOWN A BREAK

Why did I choose that word? Abandoned? Of course there's nobody out here. It's winter. It's way too cold. But how empty it all looks. How empty. Empty…Yes, empty. I'm—

Lanny felt a blow deep in his gut. He almost bent over. The muddy bottom of his river was stirring up. The clear water was gone. The bottom had come to the top and the rush of rapids was upon him, the sound of the roaring, turgid waters filling his ears.

He tried to find the raft of his reason but couldn't. The surging in his mind kept buffeting him about. Thoughts, memories—he couldn't get a hold of any one of them. The rapids swept him along, down and down along his muddy memories.

Lanny realized that he was running and showed no care for the slick sidewalk surface under his feet as he raced between the courts, slipping and sliding in his abandonment. Over and over he sprinted and skidded around the courts, unable to stop his wild momentum. He didn't know if he was running *to* something or *from* something. He had to move, and move fast. To stand still with all that was going on in his head: all the regrets, the heartaches, the denials, the feeling of uselessness that crouched in the corner of his mind—and the motherless-child-pain that lurked in the bottom of his river—all, all of it, would rise up in one gut-wrenching tide and drop on him with the hideous weight of being and having…. nothing…*NOTHING!*—

He burst into the indoor courts, the door banging loudly behind him and leaped up onto the Players Porch, blowing heavily, a harried, but barely relieved look on his face; the look of someone who had been struggling frantically in the rapids of a roiling river only to be suddenly flushed out onto a sandy bank. John, who was on the court teaching a lesson, looked up from his basket of balls with a startled expression at the sight of Lanny.

"Lanny, what the hell…. What are you doing?"

Lanny suddenly realized what he must look like and tried to grab a hold of himself.

"Oh, ah, I left the house and just went for a hike and then a jog and ended up here at the club," and he gave off a nervous snicker in between his gasps for breath. "Boy it's a long way."

And then mysteriously: "It's been such a long way," his voice trailing off, his eyes shutting for a moment. "It's been such a long way…"

"But what are you doing down here?" John asked, wanting a different answer than the one Lanny just gave, alarmed by the defeatist tone in Lanny's voice.

Lanny continued in almost a whisper, as if to himself: "Once you have given yourself over so completely to the court, so completely to the life between the lines…" and a sly chuckle came to his lips, "…a willing slave I was but I thought there would be freedom." He slowly shook his head and looked up at John who had motioned to his client on the other side of the net for a moment and had walked over to Lanny, his face full of concern.

Lanny continued, shaking his head, as if to the beat of a distant, slow tolling bell.

"I thought there would be freedom," and his voice trailed off like a wisp of smoke.

"Lanny, what the hell are saying? You sound like a—"

Again Lanny's thoughts started tumbling around in his mind and he tried to squirt out a rapid answer.

"Well, ah, as I said, I just stopped by you know. I ah, stopped by to thank that strange woman who helped me the other day and—"

"Strange? You mean Carmen?" John said calmly but still perturbed at Lanny's out-of-character behavior.

"Who?"

"Carmen."

"Oh, Yeah, Yeah. Carmen. Yeah, that's who and so…" Lanny stuttered and searched for words.

John asked: "And so?"

"And so I, I ended up…here." Again the nervous laugh.

John looked at Lanny for a moment. Something had to be wrong. This was not the calm and collected Lanny. Maybe the divorce and not talking to his father for twenty years, and the way he left tennis—all of that was finally catching up to him. John noticed how Lanny stood on the Players Porch unsteadily it seemed, rolling and unrolling his fingers as if he wanted to let go of something.

"Dude," John said, his voice worried, "are you all right? What's the matter?"

"Oh, nothing.... really." And Lanny spurted out the rest: "I just started running some sprints around the outdoor courts. Boy, it's a workout. I can tell you that."

"Running around the courts?" John asked full of disbelief.

Lanny continued at a rapid clip. "And before that I took a long hike like a I told you...geez, nature here is so beautiful, and the sunset was so.... so painful."

"Painful?"

"I mean, ah, painful because well, how many will we get to see again like that one? Maybe two, three; hell, maybe we'll never see one again. You don't know. But the sunsets just keep coming and coming, every day. And the piñon forest that stretched out before me, and the snowy mountaintops—well, you know, they, they know why they're here. They have a design, a purpose. You know?" Lanny finally finished his verbal dash.

John was trying to come to grips with Lanny's rapid barrage of words, still looking at Lanny with his big-tooth surprised look.

"Lanny, where are you going with this?"

Lanny locked a vehement gaze onto John, his fingers still unrolling but more slowly now.

"How in the hell should I know? I don't have any answers, all right?"

"All right, all right," John began soothingly, "why don't you let me take you home, right now. Or maybe we can get a beer or something. How about that? You seem a bit stressed-out, that's all; nothing weird in that, no sir. Would you like to do that? Or we could—"

"I want to watch," Lanny cut in.

"What?"

"I just want to sit here and watch. Is that ok?" And Lanny looked at John calmly, his fingers had stopped unrolling and his eyes had softened their hard edge.

Looks like he's got a hold of himself. Boy, that was weird. He seems all right though. I never thought I would see Lanny like that. Wow. I guess everybody has their moments.

John slapped Lanny on the shoulder.

"Sure, go ahead, I'll just finish up here in a half hour or so and we'll go. Sound good?"

Lanny nodded, found a chair and sat down.

John went back to his lesson. He fed a few balls and looked over at Lanny, concern on his face. Lanny lifted his hand saying he was all right.

Something made Lanny sit and wait. He couldn't get the image of the color-rich sunset out of his mind or the view of the Sangres as they must have been seen by the original native Indians, then by the first Spaniards, and now by him.

Time waits for no one, you're either with it or you're stuck. I'm stuck. I'm—

Lanny heard a loud expletive from the court on the other side and a ball came bouncing onto the platform and rolled right up to his chair. Lanny picked the ball up and looked over to the court and a couple of "sorry about that" came from the men who were playing doubles.

Lanny stood up and palmed the ball and bounced it a few times and was suddenly aware of how comforting the ball felt in his hand. It felt...right. He faintly overhead the big guy in the far court saying to his partner:

"Hey isn't that the guy who almost lost his cookies on the court hittin' on the ball machine?"

"Yeah, I think so."

"Sorry about that," Carl Holmes said as he walked over to Lanny to retrieve the ball. "Rocky," Carl pointed over at the big, florid man across the net, "he gets emotional when he double faults four straight times to lose the set. He can't hack the pressure."

"I see," Lanny nodded, a slight smile beginning as he looked over at Rocky.

"Whatever Carl is lying to you about me, don't believe it," Rocky yelled across the net. "If he's talkin' about my serve make

74

sure he tells you that he can't return it. Ain't that right, partner?" Rocky turned to his partner, Paul Bodin, and they exchanged a high five.

"That's right, big fella," Paul said slowly in his Cajun accent and then added dryly, "When you get it in."

Carl shook his head and said to Lanny loud enough so Rocky could hear, "It's easy to return Rocky's wimpy serve."

Rocky stopped in his tracks and stared at Carl in mock anger but the other guys knew Rocky and could tell he was getting pissed.

"All right, Holmes, you've got a big mouth tonight," Rocky shot back at Carl. "Let's see."

"See what? Another double fault?" Carl and his partner Alex Cole, shared a laugh and a high five.

"All right," and Rocky was fired up now. "All right, one more game. And let that man there," Rocky pointed at Lanny, "be a witness to your embarrassment."

Carl gave Lanny an apologetic look. "Well?"

Lanny hesitated but something decided for him. "Sure. Why not?"

Lanny stood next to the net post feeling amused but once the men were in position and ready to play, something sharpened in his mind.

"Good luck to ya," Rocky barked across the net and Carl just waved at him.

Rocky bounced the ball in his preparation to serve and bounced...and bounced the ball and Lanny realized that he had been counting to himself: *eight, nine, ten—*

Finally Rocky jerked up a toss and in a quick, awkward motion that belied his deliberate beginning, hammered the ball flat and hard right past Carl who could only shake his head and quip to his partner.

"Partner, did you see that good?"

Alex shrugged his shoulders and he scratched at his significant beer belly. "I don't know. I didn't really see it."

"Of course he didn't see it!" bellowed Rocky, "it was too fast!

Was that serve wimpy enough for you Carl, huh?"

Rocky and Paul shared a laugh and gave each other a high five.

"Keep it up, partner," Paul said as he took his position, "we'll be out of this game in no time."

Rocky's next serve: ten bounces and then: Whappp! Lanny winced as Rocky's serve almost took Carl's head off who stood up at the net.

Carl shouted: "Whoa!" as he ducked out of the way. "You're serving in the ad side now, right?"

Rocky was unperturbed. "Sorry. It got away from me a little bit."

"I'll say," Carl muttered.

Whappp! Double fault.

"Here we go," Carl chimed. "Now that's the Rocky we know and love."

"Don't worry, partner. You're doin' fine," Paul soothed.

Whappp!

"No! Long."

Whappp!

"Way out," Carl called gleefully. "Come on, Rocky, you can hit it harder than that."

"Yeah, come on, big dog," Alex joined in.

Lanny saw it coming: three double faults, each of Rocky's second serves hit harder than the first. Rocky took a long walk behind the baseline muttering to himself. Paul tried to go back and console his partner but Rocky waved him off.

"Wait a minute," Lanny said calmly, and he walked out on the court toward Rocky. He knew they had wanted him to just watch a friendly challenge being played out but he could never just watch tennis without his analytical mind working. That's why he could never just enjoy watching tennis when he was obsessed with it because his tennis mind was always analyzing, calculating, judging—wanting to control.

—*That's it. That's right,* he realized as he was walking on to the court.

Now, I just want to…help.

76

Rocky looked a little surprised as Lanny walked up to him.

"You have a big first serve, Rocky," Lanny began innocently.

Rocky nodded a little sheepishly but he was clearly pleased. "Thanks. I can crank one every now and then."

Pause.

Lanny rubbed his nose with his forefinger and thumb and realized that that was just the same gesture that old Professor Burns always made before he was going to tell Lanny something important on the court.

"Why do you hit your second serve so hard?"

Rocky fidgeted for a moment. "I guess because I hit every ball hard. I've always hit the ball hard."

Another pause.

Lanny smiled. "You like to hit the ball hard, don't you?"

Rocky quickly smiled back. "Yeah, I guess I do."

Pause.

"Are you a successful businessman, Rocky?" And Lanny peered intently at Rocky as if to indicate that the question was indeed a serious one.

Rocky shifted a little nervously. "I suppose I am."

"You suppose?"

More firmly. "Yes, I am. I compete very—"

"You're competitive, then?" Lanny cut in.

"Very."

"So how come you don't want to compete on the court?"

Rocky was stunned with the question and groped for an answer. Lanny continued.

"What business are you in?"

"Restaurant," Rocky said quickly and self-consciously looked past Lanny to the other guys on the court and noticed that they waited politely but were clearly intrigued by what was going on between him and Lanny.

"I bet that can be a cutthroat business."

"Not can be, it is," Rocky shot back. "I scrap to keep the overhead in line, constantly fight for business, hire, fire, change this, change that…"(into it now, a small smile begins tightly) "cry about this, that.. I do what I have to do."

"Exactly!" Lanny nodded and exclaimed, slapping Rocky on the back, and then looked directly into Rocky's eyes and slowly, under Lanny's gaze—which said he wasn't getting it— Rocky's broad smile disappeared.

"Why in the hell would you think it would be any different on the tennis court?"

Pause. And Lanny again rubbed his nose with his thumb and forefinger. Rocky absorbed what had just been said for a moment and he tried to laugh it off.

"Ah, we're talking about tennis, right?"

Lanny let a slight sigh escape from his lips. "We're talking about life…same thing, isn't it?" and Lanny arched his eyebrows rhetorically. "If you think of yourself as a competitive guy in all that you do then let's see it on the court."

Rocky scratched at the bald spot on the top of his crown and directed a questioning look at Lanny.

"Why," Lanny continued, "give your opponents so many free points with that big serve of yours? That's not being competitive, that's being egotistical. You like to show everybody how hard you hit the ball."

An ironic smile came to one corner of Rocky's mouth.

"I don't care if you have to poke that second serve, but get it in and make them play. If they beat you, they beat you. Make them earn it. Besides, you have a partner," and Lanny gestured over to Paul Bodin, "and you have to consider the best interests of the team, not yourself. You're playing doubles, not singles. So, are you man enough to poke a second serve over the net and give your team a chance to stay in the point?"

A twinkle came into Rocky's eye and his characteristically fun sense of bravado came over him. "I am," Rocky replied loudly and the other guys on the court craned their necks in his direction trying to pick up more of the conversation between him and Lanny.

Lanny didn't let up on him. "Are you ready to do what you have to do?"

"I am," Rocky declared as he expanded his chest.

All the guys on the court looked at Lanny asking with various facial expressions: what the hell did you say to him?

As Lanny walked over to Paul Bodin and said: "Do you want to help your teammate?"

"Sure do."

"Are you afraid of the ball?"

Bodin looked quickly around to see if any of the other guys had heard Lanny's question. He didn't know what Lanny was getting at.

"No."

"Then don't stand two feet behind the service line. You can't cut any balls off from back there. Get your butt up to two steps from the net and go after any ball that's within your reach, and I mean your aggressive reach. Believe me, you'll have fun up there. That's where the action is."

Lanny looked over at Carl and Alex. "Sorry for the interruption."

Carl just waved politely and Alex quipped: "No problem. But strategy won't help those dummies. Right, partner?"

"Nope," Carl replied, shaking his head.

Rocky missed his first serve wildly but did as Lanny suggested and just poked in the second serve and Alex promptly over hit it, sending the ball into the back tarp on the fly. Another soft serve and Carl miss-timed the slow speed of the ball and shanked it off the tip of his racquet, just missing Lanny, who grinned and ducked his head. Again Rocky pushed in his serve. Alex took another big swing at it and smothered the ball into the net. Now the score was ad-in. Rocky's face lit up in triumph and Bodin shouted his encouragement.

Alex tried to get Rocky's goat. "Come on, big man, what's with all the girly-serves?"

"He can't help it if you can't hit it," Bodin shot back across the net at Alex.

Rocky grinned and gestured over at Lanny. "My coach had some words of wisdom for me. "All right, here we go girls," Rocky smiled through his words. "Our ad."

Ten bounces and then: whappp! Feeling no pressure, Rocky got his big first serve in and Carl only managed to catch a piece of it and it floated over the middle and Bodin, because he was standing closer to the net, took one step and volleyed the ball away for a winner.

"Ha!" yelled Rocky. He and Bodin shared a high five and Lanny nodded approvingly and realizing that he had liked the sound of the word "coach."

"Good work, guys," Lanny said, and he felt alive, as alive as the piñon forest he had walked through earlier in the day. He savored the new feeling.

Rocky quickly walked over to Lanny and shook his hand, beaming.

"Hey thanks...?"

"Lanny. Lanny Bedford."

"Name's Rocky. Well, thanks a lot."

"You competed. I admire that," Lanny said, again nodding his head, then turned and started to walk away, he could hear the men talking behind him and a voice stopped him.

"Ah, Lanny-ah Mr. Bedford." It was Carl.

Lanny turned and Carl Holmes walked up to him.

Carl dabbed at the sweat on his forehead. "I don't know what you said to Rocky but that was pretty impressive. Rocky doesn't listen to anybody but Rocky. I never thought he could dink a serve like that. He wants to hit the ball so hard. And Bodin, you put him in real tight to the net and I felt like I didn't have enough room to get it by him."

Lanny shrugged off the compliment. "He just needed to start in a better position, that's all. And Rocky, he just needed a little conversation about what it means to compete."

"I bet you're a great teacher," Carl said with admiration in his voice and still gave his head a shake of disbelief remembering what Rocky did with his second serve. "I just can't believe you made Rocky—"

"I'm not a pro. I don't teach tennis. I—"

"But John said you were—"

"My old friend John exaggerates. I just played tennis when I was a kid. I'm actually a college teacher of English and Philosophy and I'm in between jobs right now, just moved to Santa Fe and—"

"Don't let him give you that I-just-played-when-I-was-a-kid crap," John White said with his big-tooth grin as he made his way off the Player's Porch. My friend Lanny has probably the most unique—though useless—tennis mind of anyone I have ever known or heard of and I mean Bollettieri, Billie Jean King, Gilbert, Galway, Vic Braden, Lansdorp, McEnroe—all of 'em."

"Yeah, right," Lanny shot back. "And if you believe *that* you're as dumb as John there."

"I said useless because he doesn't use it."

"I'm an academic now, John."

"John," Carl quickly jumped in, "I know we're just in the middle of December but you've already started organizing teams for the USTA season and I imagine you are pretty full with teams to coach."
Carl looked at John asking if he was right and could go on.
"That's right, Carl, I'm full," John nodded.
 "Well, the guys and I—well mostly me—were thinking of getting a team together because you know we're bored with playing each other and we'd like to give the league a shot. If you're so busy and Mr. Bedford—"

"Lanny."

"Ah, and Lanny is a sort of in between jobs," Carl continued. "Maybe he would want to coach us. I mean we're not that good really, and we'll probably get slaughtered every match, I mean we're just 3.5s, (John flashed Carl a skeptical look) but we want to give it a try but dare not do it without some coaching, because well—"

"Because we don't know what the hell we're doing," Bodin cut in with his slow cadence.

"Exactly," Carl emphasized.

"Carl," Bodin continued, "you might be a 3.5 but I know I'm not. I think—"

"I think I'm a 3.5," Rocky asserted and then looked around for support. "Alex, don't you think you are?"

"Yeah, I suppose I am."

John gave off a big laugh. "You guys aren't 3.5's. Come on, I've got some 3.5 women that would kick your butts."

All the men starting talking at once in protest, recounting match scores, stroking ability, boasts were flying. John just crossed his arms and smiled. Lanny looked at John picking up the information he needed. Finally...

"You guys are 3.0's," Lanny said quietly, flatly, and looked into the eyes of the men for a rebuttal. His tone carried authority and credibility and none of the men replied. Rocky just shuffled his feet.

"So," Carl began at last, ending the abrupt silence, "will you coach our 3.0 team?"

John wanted to pound Lanny on the back and answer for him, to get him involved in tennis again. He knew it was the only answer to get Lanny out of the crisis that seemed to be swelling up within him.

I can't do it for him. He's got to take the bait. He's got to know this would be good for him. Come on, Lanny...Do it!

"I don't know," Lanny finally said then looked for an excuse. "I've got to find a job soon so I don't think I'll—"

"We'll pay you well," Bodin chimed in and all the men looked surprised because they all knew him for a tightwad.

"Yeah," Carl added quickly. "We'll pay you more than we would pay John. No offense, John."

"None taken," and John laughed. "I knew it would only be a matter of time when Lanny here, if he wanted to teach, would get more for a lesson than the Director of Tennis but I didn't think it would be the first lesson."

"Hey, that's nice of you guys to want me to coach you but...I've never given a tennis lesson let alone coached a team," Lanny said.

"Oh, boy," John said sarcastically and rolled his eyes.

"I'm just telling them the truth, John," Lanny said firmly.

"So what?" Rocky replied in his usual blustery manner. "We've never played USTA, not one of us…I still think we're 3.5's, though,"

"You're dreaming," Bodin said and pushed at Rocky's shoulder.

"Hey, that first serve of mine is no 3.0 serve," Rocky said defiantly.

"Knock it off, guys, let the man think," Carl cut in over Bodin and Rocky.

"Look," Lanny began slowly, "I'm not your typical club pro but I think I know tennis and how it's supposed to be played and why, and as John tried to mention I do have my own way of looking at tennis and I don't know if I can teach it—"

"To a bunch of hacks like us, right Mr. Bedford?" Bodin cut in as politely as he could. Carl and Alex laughed readily and John nodded with approval but Rocky just slightly smiled. He didn't think he was a hack.

"No, I mean it. I don't know if I can teach it to anybody. I'm sure my style would be kind of old-fashioned. John has told me a lot about how the game has changed in recent years, the techniques, the racquets and so forth. So, ah—"

"So what?" Rocky cut in. "You could teach us how to compete, couldn't you? Hey, you helped me right away."

"And that was amazing," Carl had to add still surprised over what Lanny had gotten Rocky to do.

"You're damn right," Bodin agreed.

"Amazing," Alex had to say.

"Hell, I would have figured it out sooner or later," Rocky boasted.

Carl, Alex and Bodin ganged up on Rocky throwing harsh comments at him in unison.

"Yeah, a lot later than sooner," Carl managed to say above the din.

"Well, Lanny?" John wanted to force a decision on Lanny while the moment was hot.

Carl had an insight and added quickly. "We want to learn how to compete. We know you can do that. We saw it, right guys?"

Rocky, Alex, and Bodin all nodded. A murmuring of 'yep's,' 'yeah's,' and 'hell yes's' rose up.

"You all want to learn how to win? That's it?" Lanny asked.

"Hey, when you're a hacker," Bodin drawled out, "all you want to do is win, you don't care about how or with what kind of technique."

"That's right," Carl had to agree.

"But technique is very important. I don't care what level you're at. And I don't like that word 'hacker,'" Lanny said sternly. "If you guys don't think of yourselves as players, I don't think I want to waste my—"

"Yo, Bodin," Rocky cut in. "You might be a hacker but I'm sure as hell not."

"Well, Lanny," Carl began, "we might be hackers now but we want to be players. We want to know how to play and play well."

"3.0 players?" Lanny said, testing.

Carl, Bodin and Alex nodded and voiced agreement.

"What about you, Rocky?" Lanny asked wanting to put Rocky on the spot.

All the men looked at Rocky trying to compel Rocky with their facial expressions. Carl particularly glared at Rocky. But Rocky enjoyed his moment of drama. They didn't know that he was doing "it" to them again.

"A 3.0 player..." Rocky began, skeptically.

A scowl of disgust started to form on John's face and Lanny looked dead serious saying if Rocky didn't believe he was 3.0 then the deal would be off.

Rocky knew he had them and then burst out: "I'd rather be a 3.0 player than a 3.5 hack!"

Carl, Bodin, and Alex cheered Rocky's good sense then realized that Rocky had been leading them by the nose.

"Rocky, you son-of-a-bitch," Carl scoffed.

"He did it to us again," Bodin had to admit.

"He'll always be a jerk," Alex said shaking his head.

Rocky beamed, pleased with himself.

"Lanny, please don't mind the big dummy," Carl apologized. "He doesn't know any better."

"Well, Mr. Bedford, will you have us?" Bodin asked quickly.

Lanny looked at each man and then at John who said with his eyes to go ahead and do it.

"I don't want you guys to look at me like I'm some club pro and you are my clients and that you'll be paying for the typical lesson."

"I think they get that, Lanny," John said trying to close the deal.

Lanny pulled on his goatee, looked skeptically at John, and then at the men.

"It's not about the money you all will be paying me. I know I'll get a job soon enough, but I have some time left. So if I work with you guys it'll have to be on my terms and on my conditions. I know you all want to do this for fun. I understand that. So if you aren't happy with the way I do things, if one, just one of you doesn't accept the way I do things on the court then the deal is off."

Rocky couldn't hold back a giggle. "Hey come on, we're talking about playin' in a damn league."

Carl and Bodin looked at Rocky sharply wanting him to shut up.

"I mean, we're not getting ourselves into boot camp...are we?"

"Not quite," Lanny grinned. "But almost...you want to win, don't you?"

"Yeah, we want to win," Carl quickly asserted.

"Ditto," Alex said.

"That's right," Bodin agreed.

And the three men looked at Rocky saying with their faces: come on, don't be a dumb shit.

"Hell yes I want to win and win big!" Rocky said finally and smiled broadly.

"Carl," Lanny said firmly, "you'll be the captain. I will consult with you on the lineups but it'll be your call. This team will be about you guys not me. Carl, I'll give you my conditions and you can let me know if you guys approve and then we can hit the courts: asses and elbows." And he grinned at John, "I've always wanted to use that expression."

"It's appropriate for these guys."

"Yeah," Alex said. "We're all ex-military."

"I'll let you know right now, coach," Carl said. We'll accept your conditions. I'm the captain and I speak for my guys."

The deepest awareness a tennis player can have asks and answers
this basic question: What is my racquet head doing?
—Lanny Bedford, "The Long Hard Court"

"What are you talking about?" Lanny had asked John over
the phone.

"Dude, it's the Christmas Eve Canyon Road Walk. You
gotta do it. It's one of the great traditions here in Santa Fe."

"Tradition?"

"Yeah, I know you didn't hear too much of that word back
in LA where tradition means going to the same bar for a couple of
months."

"Yeah, Yeah. So what is it?"

"Look, everyone walks up and down Canyon Road singing
Christmas carols around *luminarias* and—"

"Lum,lumin-larias?"

"Small bonfires, dummy. They light them in the street in
front of the galleries and people stand around them and sing carols.
And all the sidewalks and adobe walls are lined with *farolitos*—"

"Fara-what?"

John was getting impatient. "*Farolitos*, man, you know,
those brown paper bags with candles inside that make the bags
glow—it's too cool. Look, you're going. You need to get yourself
some culture. We've been invited. My girlfriend, Yolanda, and I
will come by your house around eight. Ciao, man."

And John had hung up abruptly, not giving Lanny a
chance to ask any questions.

Invited? Hummph. Lanny thought to himself as he reached
inside the round opening of the kiva fireplace with a poker and
stirred the fire. The smell of burning piñon wood curled through
the air, its heavy sweet-pitch odor gave him a sense of
timelessness, like an ancient shaman's incense that could unlatch
the door between dimensions. He looked at his watch—*whoa,*
almost six o'clock. He had been reading all day long, rereading
many of the letters Professor Burns had written to him which the
old man had entitled: "Conversations at the Public Courts." Lanny

87

hadn't read them in over twenty years. There were over seventy of them, some as long as fifteen to twenty pages, each written in the Professor's careful, disciplined penmanship with the old-style grammar, the absence of contractions, the lack of the vernacular; long gliding sentences, page-long paragraphs that wasted not a word, fully expressing their topic sentences.

A smile tugged first at Lanny's heart and then at his face as he thought how Professor Burns wrote the same way he spoke. And as an English teacher, Lanny knew how rare that combination was because people today simply don't practice the literate skills of writing letters and being conscious about speaking clearly.

"Thoughts," Burns had said to Lanny in a letter, "are more important than emotions and good writing reflects that. In that way tennis and writing are similar. On the court it is more important what you think than how you feel. Save your feelings for before and after the match when there is no consequence. How many opponents have you seen *feel* themselves right out of a match? The only feeling that should take place on the court is the feel you have for the ball on the strings. Anything else is indulgent. Battle—that is to say tennis, is for clarity of thought, not feeling."

Lanny felt his eyes misting. He realized that when he had heard of the old Professor's death he didn't cry. Tennis and all that had gone with it had been buried deep below the muddy bottom of his river. He had merely noted it like the news of some slight acquaintance that had died.

Lanny took a deep breath and let out a guilty sigh. How he wished he could talk to the old man now, to talk about all the things that he had been too young and ignorant to understand… Finally, mercifully, a tear broke free from Lanny's eye, its salty contents full of regret, sorrow and love. It rolled down his cheek like a solemn memorial march and dropped down on the Professor's letters.

Lanny couldn't help but follow the teardrop as if the old man was summoning his attention. Lanny looked down and saw that the tear had fallen onto one of the Professor's signature sayings that he always put at the end of his letter just before he signed his name. The saying said: "Win or lose, let your last shot be your best."

Lanny couldn't remember his last tennis shot in his last match, but he knew it hadn't been his best. Hardly. It had probably been a diffident stroke, with the ball landing half way up the net. And certainly the last shot of his marriage hadn't been his best. Please. And his last shot with his father ended in a twenty—he couldn't remember exactly how long—or-so-year stalemate. And his mother, the unknown but fantasy of all fantasies that clung to his memory like the lingering physical sensation of a lost limb— her last shot had been him. How disappointed in him she would be if she…if she… Then the thought that had been hanging around his consciousness all day that he had kept at bay by all his reading leaped surely into his mind.

And now, he huffed mockingly, thinking to himself, *I'll be alone for Christmas. Some things are just deserved. This is what happens when all your last shots are your worst.*

But since he had decided to return to the court, to be in the milieu where all his best instincts and hidden wisdom came alive, a small candle, not a roaring fire, had been lit within him.

And Mom, professor, that's something, isn't it? Lanny asked out loud in his mind, demanding an answer. An arc of silence passed through Lanny as he strained his inner ear for their response and then knew what old Burns would have said: "That is not for your mother or me to answer," the Professor's bass voice sounded within him. "Besides, some questions, the most important questions, are not supposed to be answered."

But I want to be sure. I want to be sure!

Lanny could hear Professor Burns' deep chuckle resonant inside his mind. "Dear Boy, answers to the big questions are always false because one wants the security of an *answer* more than its truth. Remember what we talked about: there is no security on the court just as there is no security in life. But there *is* insecurity, there will always *be* insecurity and that's what reality is all about. So one has to—"

One has to play tennis with courage and live life with courage because courage, well, that is all we have, Lanny finished the Professor's sentence. *Yes, I remember what you said.*

A knock at the door brought Lanny out of his reverie.

"Merry Christmas, Scrooge!" John's voice bellowed from behind the front door.

Lanny cracked a smile and moved to the door and opened it. John stepped through the doorway with his girlfriend Yolanda. Snowflakes from a light snowfall blew in behind them.

John looked around in mock disbelief. "Hey, man where are the *biscochitos* and the hot chocolate!

"Bisco-what?"

"*Biscochitos,* man. Christmas cookies! You're supposed to have them ready when people come by your house during the Walk."

John looked apologetically at his girlfriend. "I'm sorry, Yolanda, he's new here. Just another gringo with no sense of tradition."

"I see," Yolanda said, faking sadness as she went along with John's ribbing. She pulled back her jacket hood and then pulled out her midnight black ponytail from under her coat that was as thick and tightly braided as the largest piece of rope Lanny had ever seen. She then smiled broadly which highlighted her high cheekbones giving hints of some native ancestry. Her face, too round to be oval, exuded the warmth of a small summer pond and her eyes, Lanny decided, were of the softest brown imaginable. Her smile was etched by two perfect dimples—and the teeth! They were, Lanny realized, the feminine version of John's. He caught himself thinking of the set of teeth the child of theirs would have.

"You guys are funny," Lanny had to admit. "As John mentioned, I'm new. Just off the bus."

"Hi, I'm Yolanda," Yolanda said before John could introduce her. Yolanda thrust out her hand and gave Lanny a hearty handshake. Lanny was surprised at her firm grip and the whipcord strength it revealed from someone so slight.

"Yolanda works at the club. She's one of the aerobics instructors," John said beaming with pride. "And dude, let me tell you she's a rock. I mean we're talkin' strong."

Yolanda rolled her eyes as if to say that John always seems to mention this to everyone he introduces her too.

"I bet she is," Lanny nodded.

"Man, you could bounce a quarter off her stomach and get it back in change," John said with the highest tone of admiration.

"John," Yolanda protested.

"Baby," and John grabbed Yolanda roughly and gave her a physical kiss. "When you're cut, you're cut... and baby, you're cut."

John raised his forearm, his hint for her to go along with their private show of affection. Yolanda looked at Lanny and then back to John asking with her eyes if it was okay. John nodded. Yolanda brought up her forearm and she and John smacked their forearms together.

Lanny could clearly see the love John had for Yolanda. John had finally met his physical equal, his tomboy woman, his workout buddy who shared his relish for physical fitness and his good-natured roughhousing. John noticed how Lanny studied Yolanda and then how he seemed to be thinking of John and Yolanda and how they were with each other. John could never resist saying things to sort of shock people. Lanny had forgotten this aspect of him.

"Yeah, dude," John began with a twinkle in his eye, "We often wrestle to see who gets to be on top."

"John!" Yolanda exclaimed, horrified and embarrassed.

Lanny looked startled, surprised by the way John had read his mind, then quickly chuckled, remembering how John was and thought that Yolanda better get used to it.

"I see she doesn't know you very well, John." And Lanny looked at Yolanda with sympathy. "Yolanda, John here has always been a loose cannon. He—"

"On and off the court!" John barked out.

"He just can't help himself."

"What, did you just get out of bed?" John exclaimed as he just noticed Lanny's disheveled hair and the wrinkled robe that Lanny half-tied to his waist.

"Oh, ah sorry, I have been reading all day and I guess I lost track of time. Let me take a quick shower and I'll be right with you."

Lanny scrambled down the small hallway and shouted over his shoulder: "Hey, John! Not that you won't but make yourself at home. There's a bottle of good Cab on the counter and some salami in the fridge. It's only three weeks old so I know it's just right for you, meat."

"Meat?" Yolanda asked. "Did he just call you meat?"

John smiled sheepishly. "Yeah. Meat. Lanny gave me that nickname when we were kids. I used to munch on hamburger patties during changeovers.

Yolanda scowled. "Gross. Why not a banana or an orange, something like that?"

"Meat," John shrugged, "it's the only thing that worked for me. Besides, chewing on that burger…well, it kind of put me in the right frame of mind if you know what I mean." And John flashed a predatory grin.

*There is tennis and there is life… Perhaps… But you can't tell **me** where the line is drawn.*
—Lanny Bedford "The Long Hard Court"

 He was near.

 All day long Carmen thought she had felt *him* brush against her and she would toss her head angrily feeling revulsion and…something else she tried to repress. It all began to radiate out from the pit of her stomach. Under her breath she cursed in Spanish.

 The last few nights she would awake and through the shadows that played across her bedroom she could see his smoky outline sitting at the end of her bed. As hard as she tried she couldn't make out his solid form through the opaque gloom or see his face, (if it really was Andrew as she suspected.) She would then lay back and after a moment remember a time—*not too long ago!* when, in this same bed, the bed of her childhood, she had unconsciously flexed and relaxed her limbs while feelings of innocence and desire moved through her body like a new awareness. And now she did not have to lie in the secrecy of her room for those feelings to visit her. They were with her like an extra sensation; like a shadow she could feel as it lay across her waist.

 Damn it all. I've had it with these…silly thoughts! She shouted inwardly, angrily, and pushed down heavily on the gas pedal. Driving home from work she sped down Old Santa Fe Trail bumper-hugging anyone in front of her. *Que pinche traffico!* She scowled with the memory of a time when cars didn't line up from Paseo de Peralta all the way to Cordova; a time when there wasn't really any before and after work traffic in town except on Cerrillos, and that was because of all the through traffic from Albuquerque to Espanola and Taos that had to go right through Santa Fe. And now all of the out-of-town license plates! All those cars going seemingly nowhere, going slowly, the people in them, their faces gawking at the adobe houses as if they hadn't already seen a thousand of them since they had arrived in Santa Fe. *Come on! Let's go!*

Stopping at a light she looked down Cordova and she was almost startled to suddenly notice that some of the homes bordering the street were outlined with a blaze of Christmas lights. She realized then that she had not been buoyed by the festive atmosphere of the Christmas season and tonight was Christmas Eve! She couldn't remember why this would be the first Christmas Eve that she hadn't wanted to take the Walk. Most of her brothers and sisters and their families would be going and she had thought: *Who needs old Auntie Carmen tagging along?*

But her friend Yolanda had talked her into going on the Canyon Road Walk. Yolanda, (*boy she can be so annoying),* had insisted Carmen meet up with her and her boyfriend, John. It seemed like Yolanda had always been able to insist on what they would do together ever since they were little girls. Carmen decided that Yolanda and John were meant for each other, like two wolves, an alpha male and an alpha female, attracted to each other because no other available mate was tough enough. The brief thought about John made her—despite her initial resistance—think about his friend Lanny and the way his blue eyes had looked at her and, from a corner of her mind, continued to look at her. Inwardly she saw those eyes were there studying her—*damn him!* And also they were full of a male's admiration, her feminine instinct told her. She thought: *Poor guy, that day he had seen my body from every angle in the mirror's reflections and **that** certainly stopped the way he was studying me so coolly.* Something deep within her felt a twinge of victory.

Yes, he needed to look at me that way, didn't he? But I don't need to see him that way. And all the talk about stretching made him squirm, didn't it?

Rather than mollifying her, these thoughts made her angry. *Why? Why?*

And why did she have to dwell on how it felt to cradle his head in her hands while he lay on the court that day so vulnerable, struggling for consciousness? The feeling of his hair between her fingers had been so…secretly intimate. And when he finally opened his eyes—she couldn't forget his look of discovery that made her feel like she had been really looked at for the first time and it had struck her like a thunderbolt.

She squeezed the steering wheel and looked away from the festively decorated houses and thought how she just wanted Christmas to come and go quickly. Sure there would be the family gatherings that in the past had brought her such contentment and joy and *protection—yes they had*—but she thought she could find excuses not to attend most of them this time around.

Finally she made it home and dashed up the stairs, pulling on the heavy wooden and wrought iron stair railing, throwing a greeting to her dad over her shoulder. She felt too bothered to exchange any small talk but did feel a twinge of guilt knowing that her father was not well and she should have looked in on him.

She flung open the door to her bedroom, closed and locked it behind her.

He was near. *I always feel his shadow first.*

Her father and brothers had knocked out an adobe wall to combine two rooms and a bathroom into the same room to give Carmen privacy and enough space for a workout area for those clients who preferred to come to her house for yoga, aerobics, spinning, and light weight work. On the wall just past the doorway hung a large colonial Spanish weaving with its beautiful reds, yellows, greens and blacks, branching out from a central diamond motif, with jagged lines, some basic stripes and lozenges. She walked passed it without a glance. She continued on, passing her territorial canopied bed of dark, magenta-colored bedding, the same bed her great-grandparents had slept in for over seventy years, and where her father and his seven siblings had been born. She walked by the large nineteenth-century chest-on-legs with ornate chip-carvings, and started to shed her clothing. Continuing through her workout area, a large wall mirror showed her impatiently pulling off her cross-training Nikes while she hopped on one foot and then the other. As she entered the bathroom, she had left a trail of warm-up pants, shoes, socks, shirt, bra and panties. She started the bath. She watched the water tumble out of the faucet and the vapors of steam rise up. She ran her hand under the flow of water and let the steam billow across her face as she closed her eyes, looking inward for a quiet space…

He was near.

Damn it!

His assault on her consciousness felt dangerous—*it must be Andrew,* but what if it wasn't? And at the same time she felt a need. Was it just flesh reaching for flesh? *Oh, isn't that ridiculous!*

She put her hair up and took a glimpse at the bathroom mirror and knew that she would see her face revealing the conflict within her and then had to admit to herself as she rubbed the ivory skin of her thigh: *It could be so easy. I could take a lover any time I want. But I swore—boy did I swear—to abstinence. I didn't want to be touched after…that. And now I want my… skin to lie against???*

He was very near.

Looking for relief Carmen slid under the hot water of the tub, exhaled a long sigh, and then watched the suds of her bubble bath trying to cling to her breasts and her private parts in an attempt to affirm her modesty.

After a couple of minutes the heat of the water had created a feeling of lethargy, but under her skin she was agitated. She waited for the warm bath to win out over her anxiousness. She tried to busy her mind with the details of the day and other such trivia but the steady drip of the water kept getting louder, pulling her back to *that* memory, magnifying the awareness of everything that had happened.

Carmen blew through her lips in disgust and rose up abruptly out of the foaming tub. She got up so quickly that the suds fell away from her body. Dripping from the bath she walked out of the bathroom, wet and naked, and over to her workout area. She opened a large, squat, ornate wood and tin pie safe that had, over two hundred years ago, kept all the valuables of her family. She now used it to store her workout equipment. She poked around impatiently, finally pulling out a stair-step and began a vigorous step aerobics routine.

That's it!!! I am going to exercise until I drop. I'll cleanse my mind and exhaust my body.

The love of tennis is not like the love for a woman ... it's much deeper than that. When was the last time a woman gave you a real identity?

—Lanny Bedford, 'The Long Hard Court'

Lanny was hardly prepared for what greeted him as he left his adobe *casita* with John and his girlfriend, Yolanda. It was as if he had stepped into an idealized postcard that captured the unique southwest charm, tradition and the festive nostalgia of a more authentic Christmas Eve past. The small alleyway that led to Canyon Road was lined with *farolitos* that glowed and flickered in the frosty dark beckoning to them. Lanny felt...lured—*that's it*— lured along this trail bracketed with dancing light, and a kernel of awareness started to open within a deep corner of his mind suggesting that he was on a journey. A kind of journey you suddenly discover you're on but you don't know when it began or where it is supposed to end. Was it a journey you thought you were taking or was *something* taking you?

Lanny thought to himself: *A journey for tonight? Or what?* He then remembered those times on the court when something— that's the only word for it because he could never come up with a better one—something had led him from point to point, break to break, set to set, with its own agenda and he was just along for the ride.

As they neared the end of the alley where it led out onto Canyon Road, Lanny turned to look back and was again reminded of how his little adobe looked like a gingerbread house with frosting around the trim of the square roof and along the tops of the rounded walls. It sat there at the gray shadowy end of the *Callita, de Los Cincos Pintores,* the little alley way named for the five painters who came to Santa Fe in the early 1940's and began an artist colony and lived and painted in their adobe residences on and around Canyon Road. The locals called them "the five nuts in the five mud huts." (At one point Lanny's adobe had been used, along with its other colorful uses, as a storage space for painting supplies and canvases). Lanny's eyes were attracted to the way the starlight and the flickering light of the *farolitos* reflected off the charcoal darkened inset windows of the adobe house and to its earthen walls that seemed to have risen right up out of the ground by some seismic disturbance, and were there to remain like a small monolith of endurance that could easily shrug off the centuries.

Lanny sighed. *A thousand bucks a month rent is still too much, even for all the history that comes with it. But it has taught me a few things, hasn't it? What more is it going to make me let go of?*

As they stepped into the street, Lanny turned around and saw John's big-toothed grin under the light of a *farolito* that perched above him on a wall bordering the street. John's face glowed as brightly as the lights around him and he seemed like a little kid looking at a Christmas tree with presents overflowing out from underneath its branches.

"Is this too cool or what!" John exclaimed. "You can't get this in L.A., can you?"

Lanny looked down the street and saw *luminarios* dotting the street all the way down to *Paseo de Peralta* and the dark clumps of people who were gathered around them singing. The sound of many-voiced Christmas carols drifted up the street to him and the welcoming smell of burning piñon wood infused the air. All the streetlights and glaring residential porch lights had been turned off. The street was lit by thousands of candles and bonfires, evoking a scene from the street's distant past. The alternating flicker of light and striped shadows thrown off by darting flames muted all colors, and Lanny felt like he was on the set of some black and white film shot by Gabriel Figueroa, Mexico's greatest cinematographer.

"Man, it's beautiful," Lanny breathed.

They moved down the street through the stream of people who were all in high spirits: families, parents with baby strollers, couples. Many had put blinking red and green lights on their hats. Yolanda said: "My grandmother lived up at the top of Canyon Road before most of the (and she smiled at John) gringos came here and turned it into a street for rich people and tourists and artsy-fartsy types."

Yolanda grinned mischievously at John who just smiled and nodded as if to encourage her to continue. Lanny could hardly make out her face in the darkness but could see the intermittent whiteness of her teeth as she spoke from under her parka hood.

"My uncle, who is a lot older than my dad, told me," Yolanda began, "that when he was a small kid there were no artists around. There were people who made things and did art—if you will—but they weren't called artists. They made what they made out of tradition, not from a bunch of ideas that they got in a French art school. In fact," she almost whispered to Lanny, "you may meet one of those people, who we call a *Santero* tonight," and a bright line of white looked up at him.

"Anyway," Yolanda said picking up her volume and tempo, "my father and my aunt used to run up and down this street when they were small kids on Christmas Eve stuffing themselves with *posole and biscochitos* and staying ahead of *La Posada* and trying not to get caught by the *Chupacabre* who wanted to take their cookies." And she laughed, delighted at her own story.

"What's a chuppa—"

"Dude," John cut in, "forget it. You don't want to get her started with all those fairy-tales and ghost stories. I don't know where the hell she got them from."

"Everyone in my family can tell a story. It's normal," Yolanda said in a matter of fact tone.

They were passing a Gallery whose name Lanny couldn't pronounce. The walkway to the gallery was lined with *farolitos* and the barren branches of the tree in the front were covered in string lights. Lanny could see through the windows that the gallery specialized in paintings done in watercolors.

"Hey, want to check out some art? Maybe they have some hot chocolate and some cookies in there," John said hungrily. "Looking at bad art always makes me hungry."

"Not now," and Yolanda tugged at John's arm. "We have to meet up with Carmen down where that big *luminario* is, see?"

About a block and a half down Lanny could see a fairly large bonfire partly obscured by people. He could see some glowing embers floating up from the flames.

"Carmen?" Lanny asked, surprised, a slight tone of wariness in his voice.

"Yes, Carmen," Yolanda said quickly with as much innocence in her voice as she could muster. "She invited us. You know her, don't you?" Again, the innocent tone.

Lanny paused and thought about his encounter with Carmen in the yoga room and the underlying tension that had been present. But the passing days had made him reinterpret their *mano a mano* and he decided that after all he had liked the tension between them. He decided that he had no expectations, no obligations, and the needs he did have he would not hide. He would be an open book. He would be a conduit of fate and truth.

Girded by these thoughts, Lanny said with a hint of a smile and some sarcasm: "I don't think Carmen likes me. Are you sure her invitation included me?"

Lanny saw a flash of white teeth as Yolanda looked up at him from under her hood. She read the hint of mockery in Lanny's voice and she called him on it.

"Does it matter whether she did or not? I mean, if you are uncomfortable, I understand. Carmen is a beautiful woman and some men are, well—"

"Just afraid of her," John cut in, having to get a word in. "There's no question, dude, I've seen her around some guys and well, it doesn't go well for them. She kind of enjoys it to, doesn't she, babe?" He then laughed and Yolanda joined him.

"Yeah, she gets hit on so much that she can be pretty short with guys and pretty cynical, so she makes fun of them sometimes."

"I see," Lanny said, unimpressed.

"Don't worry," Yolanda said and she playfully punched Lanny in the shoulder, "I'll make her behave herself."

"By all means," Lanny said with a smile, "let her be herself. I'm a big boy."

John laughed saying with his eyes that Lanny's apparent confidence was mistaken.

"Whatever you do, dude, don't let her catch you looking at her body."

Yolanda couldn't suppress a giggle. "Don't worry, it'll be all right. She'll be polite. Anyway, she's probably not your type and I think I know you're not her type."

"What she's saying is," John said with his big-toothed grin, "that she doesn't like...*gringos*," John said the last word with relish, trying as best he could to say it with a Spanish accent.

Lanny put on his best Buddha face and said: "Whatever happens, happens."

On the court the tennis player's psychology is basically one of selflessness. The self doesn't matter. The only psychology a player has to be concerned with is that of the opponent. Everything a player needs to know and needs to be aware of is on the other side of the net.

—At The Public Courts: Conversations with the Professor, alias "The Pusher."

Carmen stepped out into the dry cold air and headed down Acequia Madre to Delgado Street then over to Canyon Road. Her calves and hamstrings quivered with fatigue, and the skin of her forehead and cheeks still showed the red glow of her exertions. But she felt the calm induced by tired muscles and by the all the coital- type energy she had spent during the furious pace of her exercise.

She welcomed the augury cold breeze that blew up against her face, allowing the wind of the high desert to renew her state of mind. With all the lights off in the neighborhood, above her a speckled freshet of stars poured through the inky black backdrop of night. She smiled as she noticed a glowing angel-kite that someone had sent up to hover with benediction above Canyon Road.

She moved through the streets of her childhood feeling a comfort from intimately knowing all the darkened shapes of the houses around her. She anticipated the curve of a wall before she saw it, knowing without looking down where she needed to place her foot to remain on level footing. Her mind nodded with the knowledge of what all the gardens and yards behind the thick adobe walls looked like because she had played in every one of them.

At least, of course, she reminded herself, *what they used to look like.*

The adobe architecture of the homes that embraced the street accommodated the surrounding environment rather than imposing foreign shapes, angles, and material. It…belonged there: unpretentious, maternal and grounded, grounded in the past. She had always taken "adobes" as a given, like the Sangres that rose up above her house. But tonight she understood how the shapes around her provided a deep sense of comfort, continuity, and stability. And she remembered a poem her brother had written while he was restoring an old adobe on some family land in Tesuque.

Hear the bricks, the skin
Of God, drying in the sun,
Orphaned squares
Of ancient
Earth mix,
The source of the first
And last habitat.
Feel the adobe wall,
The wide hide
Of clay
That seals off
Rogue winters
And the mandate
Of heat, sun,
And fire.
Tomb, womb
For whomever
Seeks elements
Of earth like a
Lover who loves
To pack, pound
And trawl away
While adobe sighs.

The words filled her with understanding and went right to her heart, her adobe heart. Manny restored the adobe—part home, part fortified outpost—that had been built by the family in the 1800's. It stood on some property in Tesuque that had been used for sheep grazing. Its two and a half foot adobe walls remained hearty and defiant, though some patching needed to be done. The last family members to live in the house, some seventy years ago, had tried to "modernize" it because hardened dirt floors and vigas were for poor people. So Manny had torn up the wooden planks that covered the deer blood and straw floor and removed the false roof that covered the raw cut vigas. Manny was the historian of the family. He had an interest in collecting all of the Villafuerte family's oral history and papers and letters of historical interest of the family that had established itself in Santa Fe along with the original founding families over three hundred years ago.

She turned back to look at her street with nostalgia and sadness. Now only a few of the old Hispanic families remained on the block where Carmen grew up. But because of historical preservation ordinances that applied to her neighborhood, none of the new Anglo owners could change the architecture of the houses they had bought. She shook her head, remembering part of a conversation between her mother and father that she had overheard. They had sat talking, as always, at the breakfast table a couple of weeks ago, their conversation was a combination of English and Spanish. Carmen had lingered in the hallway to smell the fresh coffee and flash-fried *sopapillas*: smells that took her back to her earliest childhood memories She noted then that the older her parents became, the more Spanish they would use when they spoke to one another, pushing more and more of the English words out of their sentences. Carmen imagined that this language was probably the one of their courtship and they both seemed compelled to return back to a time when their youthful affections were immediate and intense. They both needed the comfort of summoning up those ways of speaking when their lips and hands had followed their words.

In the conversation her father had said, between bites (and pauses) while he carefully laid down a line of honey on the next part of the *sopapilla* where he would take a bite, that when he went out to get the mail, there was this man in snakeskin cowboy boots who had on a very pressed shirt with Southwest designs on it. He was standing there looking at the house. His face looked like it had been scrubbed too hard, her father had said, and he had a look in his eyes that her father had seen before and he knew the question that was on the man's mind.

Her father had told the man:

"My family built most of this house before the 1848 Treaty of Guadalupe Hidalgo—"

"I knew it!" the man had gushed, his scrubbed face glowing red with envy.

Carmen's father had continued while chewing saying to the man that we considered ourselves Spaniards; that we didn't and don't like the damn Mexicans or (smile) the land-grubbing gringos. And finished by saying that his grandfather added more rooms to the house, making the adobe brick by hand. He built the kiva fireplace himself and no, it's not for sale.

"How'd you know I was interested in buying your house?" the man had asked with surprise, "Mr.? Mr.?"

"Villafuerte. Manuel Faustino Ortiz y Villafuerte. I have seen many like you before. You are hungry for history. I see it in your eyes," Carmen's father had said in a matter of fact tone. "Why do you go around trying to buy other people's history?

"Look, I'll give you top dollar," the man had said as if he hadn't heard Carmen's father and continued to smile through his words, "or any dollar you'd like. You name it."

Carmen's father stopped his tale and looked up from his *sopapilla* and in a goofy manner began to role his eyes that after forty some years his wife still felt was funny. They shared a chucked then:

"Gringos!" Manuel continued in mock horror. He said he squinted disapprovingly at the man, who continued his vacant smile, somehow proud of his new southwestern identity. Manuel hitched up his pants and left his hands on his hips.

"I am sure it is hard for you to understand, but some things aren't for sale. There is a small family cemetery behind the house. My great-grandfather is buried there among others of my family. My father was born and died in that house. One day, I, too will die in that house. There are family heirlooms, belongings, painted portraits, photographs, and diaries going back over two centuries in that house. The memories of my ancestors are in that house. It is not a piece of real estate."

The man nodded his head, (that smile again) and dug a toe of his snakeskin boot in the ground and after a moment of digging, dislodged a stone.

"In time, Mr. Bee-ah-fort-ta, everything is just real estate…Enjoy your home."

Carmen remembered that when her father related the last thing the man had said that her parents suddenly sat in silence except for the sound of tinkling forks and knives.

She buttoned the top collar of her coat against the cold wind that blew in from the northeast through the snow packed Sangre de Cristo Mountains and then down upon Santa Fe like an invisible blanket of chilled air. She shook her head, remembering the conversation between her parents and thought that she could very well inherit the house when her parents died. But she, like her father, would never sell.

She approached the big luminario at the corner of Delgado Street and Canyon Road where she would meet up with Yolanda, John, and a friend Yolanda said she was bringing. She could hear 'Silent Night' being sung and it lifted her spirits. A crowd of about fifteen people stood around the fire singing, some off key, Carmen noted, and she smiled to herself. A man with a lighted reindeer hat on handed her a Dixie cup with hot apple cider while saying:

"Merry Christmas. The Peterson-Spielberg Fine Arts Gallery invites you to come in and see our beautiful artwork."

"Thank you. Perhaps I will," Carmen replied as she looked up at the gallery that was perched on the corner of the street, just up a small flight of stairs. The gallery used to be a house, she knew, *Abuelita* Delgado's house. She remembered how delicious the old lady's flat, red chile enchiladas had been. On Fridays after school let out, *Abuelita* Delgado always had a batch of flat enchiladas for the kids who had worked so hard at school all week: *"Estudiando muy dura, toda la semana, verdad, mi 'jita?"* the old lady would say in her sing-song voice. And Carmen would answer her in English and Spanish: "Yes, *Abuelita, yo he trabajado* very hard all week."

A tide of well-being began to rise up within her. She began to hum along with the song. She glanced around the fire and could hardly make out the singing faces obscured by the flickering shadows cast about by the flames of the bonfire. The song, mournful yet joyous, began to fill the quiet around her.

Then, there it was...'that feeling'. It looked at her.

Looking around she didn't notice any faces hooded by parkas or heads framed by earmuffs that glanced in her direction. Something made her look directly across the fire through the rising smoke and floating embers. The smoky outline of a pair of eyes with a glint of moonlight in them stared at her. Slowly, an animal attraction made her eyes stare back as she probed the nature of the admiration and male intent cast out by those eyes across the flames. She could feel her pulse quicken as her body became alert under her winter clothing.

Standing in front of the bonfire, Lanny extended his hands and felt the warmth of the blaze course though his gloved hands. He closed his eyes and let the peace of the song pass through him. When he opened his eyes, his eyes found hers, just like hers had found his on that day when he laid on the court, his head cradled in her hands. And again, it seemed like a dream to him. Through the anonymity of the smoke and sparks he felt he could look at her eyes with all of his truth.

"Hey, girl!" Yolanda's elbow dug into Carmen's side.

"Oh."

"Did I startle you?" Yolanda asked squeezing Carmen's arm.

Carmen quickly looked back across the fire. The eyes had vanished.

Carmen recovered and smiled quickly. "I was just trying to remember all the words to 'Silent Night.' I guess I have forgotten most of them."

"Hi, Carmen," John said as he came up on the other side of Carmen. "Merry Christmas."

"Merry Christmas, John. I see Yolanda was able to drag you out here in the cold."

"Drag me? Hell, I wouldn't miss it. There was never anything like this where I grew up. It's too cool. Right, Lanny?"

Lanny moved out of the deeper shadows and into the light of the fire next to John.

"It's very charming." And Lanny looked at Carmen. "Even beautiful."

Carmen's eyes flashed briefly which told Lanny that she knew he was referring to her. Yolanda and John didn't pick up on the subtle reference. Carmen looked quickly away from Lanny and Lanny realized that their secret communication had begun.

But where would it lead?

"I see you appreciate our tradition," Carmen said quickly giving the word "appreciate" a slight accusatory tone.

"Indeed I do," Lanny replied, unblinking, studying her.

I hate that look, Carmen reminded herself.

"How could he not?" John jumped in innocently. "He's from LA."

Carmen cocked her head with a look that said she knew all about Lanny.

"You—"

"Lanny," Lanny cut in calmly, a slight smile coming through his goatee. "You can call me Lanny."

Carmen went right ahead, ignoring Lanny's request.

"We also have other traditions here that you might not be so easily *charmed* by," Carmen said hoping Lanny could discern the slight edge in her voice. "If you are a good student, if you are bright enough, perhaps I could teach some of them to you."

Yolanda caught Carmen's tone and her strong teeth smiled at Lanny saying: "I told you so."

"Lanny here has a Master's degree, Carmen," John gushed not aware of the undertones in Carmen's words. "A real professor, huh, Lanny? Mr. Bookworm. That's Lanny."

"A real professor?" Carmen asked, mock surprise in her voice.

Lanny shrugged apologetically. "So I've been told."

Carmen nodded her head with a look of almost, but not quite, pity. Lanny marveled at her subtlety.

"All that studying and book learning. Tell me, professor, have you realized that you now have to unlearn everything? That life, I mean real life, makes your beloved books seem rather irrelevant?"

For a moment Lanny fought down the shock that somehow she *knew* all about him. He felt naked. Unnerved. He hoped to hell Carmen couldn't see him fumbling for his composure.

"I guess you could argue that, but—"

Yolanda's half-suppressed giggle saved Lanny.

"Come on let's walk, let's sing."

"Yeah," John chimed in. "Let's be merry."

Yolanda took Carmen arm in arm and they walked ahead of John and Lanny.

Yolanda turned her head to Carmen and smiled impishly. Carmen replied with an annoyed frown. A couple of more steps and Carmen looked at Yolanda who still had that smile on her face. They both burst out laughing.

"Why did you have to bring *him* along?" Carmen said, impatiently flickering a strand of hair off her forehead.

Yolanda squeezed Carmen's arm and the impish grin went from her mouth to her eyes.

"Well, he seems kind of cocky and we both know that you're cocky. So—"

"So. So what?"

"So, I thought it would be fun."

"I am not here to entertain you."

"You always do. Besides, he's new in town and John really wants to get him out to meet people and to (big smile) check out some of our *traditions.*

"But after the Walk we're going to my house for *posole* and—"

"Your mother's handmade corn tortillas," Yolanda gushed. "I can't wait."

"She just made them because you were coming, you brat," Carmen scolded through a smile.

"It'll be all right. John's friend is okay. He's cute but maybe a bit annoying.

Yolanda noticed Carmen's quick frown.

"But he is cute, don't you think?"

"Yeah, in a gringo kind of way, but don't even think about trying to set him up with me. Besides, (and Carmen thought she could feel Lanny's eyes looking at her from behind) I don't like his look, and he presumes too much. So don't—"

"All right already. Do me a favor and just be polite. He's harmless."

"So *you* think," Carmen said sharply as she glanced over her shoulder to see John and Lanny pointing and gesturing, taking in the scenes around them. She noticed that they were walking between two large galleries on either side of the street. Both had huge picture windows in front. The reflection off both darkened windows put the four of them in a momentary blaze of flickering light given off by hundreds of *farolitos* and two opposite roaring *luminarios*. In the brief second of illumination, like the bright flash of light given off by a sudden bolt of lightning, she saw Lanny's eyes seeking hers in the reflection.

Ultimately, and I mean ultimately, it didn't matter if I won or lost. I was obsessed with my feel for the ball. If I lost but the ball had felt like a raindrop dissolving in my palm I was secretly elated, though I pouted for my father's benefit. If I won but the ball felt like a rock, I was as discouraged as any loser.
—Lanny Bedford, "The Long Hard Court"

They crossed over a stone bridge in front of Carmen's house that spanned over the *Acequia Madre.* The 'Mother Ditch' was part of a system of irrigation dug by the Spaniards over three hundred years ago in order to provide vital water for the fledging colonial settlement of Santa Fe. The bridge narrowed at the end, funneling down to a heavy wooden gate/door that had a thick iron bar window. It was embedded in a thick, fortress-like adobe wall that stood eight feet tall, smooth and rounded. The moon frosted the top of the wall and Lanny noticed how gray and black shadows played across it giving it a hint of movement, like a massive brown adobe wave getting ready to wash down over them.

"Cool bridge, huh, Lanny?" John's breath puffed out in front of him. "It's all stone."

The moon had come out from behind a shutter of clouds and Lanny could see that the cobblestones under his feet had been worn down and wondered how much foot-traffic could have caused the smooth-wearing of the stones.

Walking ahead with Yolanda, Carmen said over her shoulder:

"For a hundred years or so this bridge used to be the main entrance to the house. My Grandfather had narrowed the bridge at the end and turned the big gate entrance into just a door. But it wasn't big enough or strong enough for cars so he built a bigger bridge over there (she gestured to her left). This bridge had been just for people, horses and wagons."

With some effort Carmen pushed open the heavy door that led into a wide courtyard. Lanny could hear its old, rusting, weathered hinges complain, the deep creaking sounds evoking a pre-modern past of wood, stone, adobe, forged iron and the echo of horses' hooves moving across the bridge.

"Get a load of these walls, Lan," John gushed as he extended his arms to measure the width of the wall. "Over two feet at least. How charming and beautiful. And what privacy. Nobody can see in here from the street. Just beautiful. Don't you think?"

Lanny agreed, still hearing horses on the bridge. "It sure is."

"People always say that now," Carmen began in a matter of fact tone, "but this wall wasn't built for privacy or to be charming. It was built simply for protection against hostile attacks. It was still wild around here back then."

"That which was practical is now an aesthetic," Lanny said while he formed the thought in his mind.

"Good deduction, professor," Carmen said with amused sarcasm.

"Yes it's 'The Santa Fe Style'," Yolanda said, echoing Carmen.

"A new style," Carmen giggled, still walking arm in arm with Yolanda, "just recently discovered by Anglos about twenty years ago. Discovered..."

Carmen looked over her shoulder at Lanny. His face was illuminated by the house lights coming through the front window as they approached the porch. He peered back at her, blue eyes unblinking.

"A dangerous word don't you think, professor?"

"You tell me, young lady," Lanny said in his most professorial tone.

"My Spanish ancestors said they *discovered* a new world but it was a very old world and the indigenous peoples didn't need to be discovered. They knew who they were and where they lived.

"And?" Lanny wanted her to get to the point.

They all stepped up to the porch, which was covered by a portal supported by thick wooded posts with ornate Spanish carvings. Carmen turned fully around and looked at Lanny, her eyebrows arched with the fullness of her thought and she cocked her head to one side. Lanny figured that gesture was meant to signal her disapproval. He took in her whole stance and despite the winter clothes, the sensuality of her bodily curves and athletically toned muscles seemed to move under her clothes slowly with an uncoiling potential that forced him to stare, unwilling to miss her slightest movement. He attempted to hide behind a smile and tried to look at her with as much a sense of discovery as he could.

"Well, when you say you've discovered something, that means you can take it for your own. For example, (and Carmen boldly reached around Lanny's waist and took his wallet from his back pocket and held it up, her eyes narrowing for an instant as if to tell him to stop *that look* of his) this wallet, your wallet you would say, well, I'm going to take it and I'm not stealing it. No, didn't steal it, I *discovered* it."

"So you're saying that Anglos have stolen the Santa Fe Style?"

"You're a very good student. You get an 'A'."

Yolanda giggled and punched Carmen in the arm.

"Like always, she exaggerates. Actually, Anglos have paid good money, sometimes ridiculous money, to have the Santa Fe Style. I'm expensive aren't I, baby?"

John showed his teeth. "Let me count the ways."

Carmen opened the arched front door and gestured for everyone to come in.

"*Mi casa es su casa.*"

"And that also means all of your mom's handmade corn tortillas," Yolanda said as she moved through the doorway.

Lanny stepped past Carmen and he glanced at her hostess' welcoming smile that was more (he knew and she knew) of a smirk than a smile, and he couldn't help saying with a quick flash of his eyes: yes I know you want to be the teacher, you want to be in control, you want to be on top, so to speak, and no, I'm not chastened…I like you.

Carmen studied Lanny's back as he passed by her. *Is he dumb or just a smart-ass?* she wondered. *Why did I let him into my house? Is he dangerous?....Yes....But...Am I dangerous too?...Yes, damn it...Yes.*

They made their way across a well-worn though carefully polished *Saltillo* floor that led from a small foyer into the living room. Dusky, mud-yellow walls, pock-marked with *nichos* containing old family heirlooms, rose up to a high ceiling crossed by thick vigas that were supported by elegant, carved and painted corbels. In between the vigas, was a herringbone pattern of bone-white *latillas*. A Christmas tree decorated in red chile lights and handmade religious ornaments stood in front of one picture window. A huge kiva fireplace dominated one corner of the room. Lanny could see that the raised hearth of the fireplace was deep. Looking through its rounded opening and into the piñon blaze, he figured there was room for a couple of logs four feet in length. The smooth, trawled surface of the kiva hinted at the hand-made nature of the construction. Next to the kiva, just off to the side, stood a large, nineteenth-century six-board *trastero,* its top lined with painted woodcarvings of *santos*. The smell of boiling posole floated in from a curved hallway to their left. On the wall next to the kiva was an impressive tapestry with the Villafuerte coat of arms on it: a blood-red crescent moon hovering above a floating armored helmet, surrounded by three mailed fists clutching daggers and two rearing white stallions underneath. And then Lanny stopped in his tracks, as he saw a cross on the opposite wall. John, too, came to a stop, bumping into Lanny as they looked up at the cross that was easily eight feet in height. It was a wooden cross painted in black lacquer—but the light of it, the brilliant gold light coming off it made Lanny squint. He released a low breath and John echoed him. The thought jumped into Lanny's mind that this cross could make a non-believer drop to his knees. A full minute went by as Lanny and John took in the story depicted on the cross. Lanny had seen crosses all over Europe, and Mexico, great crosses of gold, silver, crosses inlaid with gems, ivory, mother-of-pearl, but nothing could touch this cross's evocation of a miracle and a simple, yet profound, expression of devotion. *God, it seems like gold!* He had to remind himself that the figures and the scenes depicted on the cross were made of straw and not gold.

A voice cleared itself as if trying to build up enough strength to talk. "I see you like my cross. It took me six months to make it…"It nearly killed me," the voice said with a weak but gruff laugh.

"Oh, daddy, you're up. Did we wake you coming in?" Carmen asked with concern in her voice as she walked over to her father, Manuel, and embraced him.

"No, no, 'hita, I was just sitting here by the fire."

Carmen was shocked to realize that her father was shrinking before her very eyes. The chair next to the fire could never have hid him a year ago, but now the chair swallowed him as if he were a child. His pants, held up by suspenders, sagged on him. His checkered flannel shirt hung loosely around him, and from his head, tuffs of stubborn white hair stood up above the surrounding gray. His skin seemed to hang wearily on him but his black eyes, though watery, had a shine to them that revealed an intense vitality.

"Yes," the old man continued, his lips moving before his words were heard as if his lips needed to gather momentum before he could utter a sound. "Yes, I was just sitting by the fire thinking about time and how (bitter-sweet smile) time ruins us all."

Pause.

"Ah, Daddy," Carmen began anxiously filling in the silence, "this is Yolanda's friend John and his friend (pause) Lanny."

Manuel shook John's hand, nodding and then Lanny's and Lanny was surprised at the supple strength in Manuel's grip. Despite the polite look of casual interest in Manuel's eyes, Lanny thought the old man was also studying him at the same time.

"Nice to meet you Mr. Villafuerte and yes, I am most impressed, even…emotional—and I'm sure that's the right word— about your cross. I see you have put all the Stations of the Cross on it in such an intricate and detailed way. The narrative of the straw is deeply moving. The cross…speaks."

"You are perceptive," the old man said, his facial expression coming alive while his foggy eyes smiled.

"It's astonishing," Lanny continued. "And standing from here I would swear that the cross is inlayed with gold, not straw. It shows a hand of (and Lanny looked at Carmen for a moment and then back to Manuel) deep passion, rather than just art."

Manuel's forehead knotted with interest as his hands pulled at the corners of his mouth.

"Yes...why yes," the old man's voice began in a surprised tone: "Ah, so you...feel my motivation?"

Speaking modestly, Lanny replied: "Perhaps on one level I do."

"I think it is my last Passion and I thank God he gave me the time and the strength to complete it."

"Oh, daddy, don't talk like that," Carmen said, her voice betraying her irritation and sadness. "There is plenty more where that one came from. I am sure you'll start a new one any day now and next year at the Spanish Market you'll win first prize again."

An insight struck Lanny and he couldn't help what came out of his mouth.

"It's okay, isn't it Mr. Villafuerte, that this kind of religious devotion and expression has only one moment, one shape? That it is the only gift of its kind?"

The old man's eyes quickened and a knowing smile spread across his face.

"Ah, you *do* know my motivation.*"

Again being modest. "Perhaps."

"Well I know it is beautiful, too," John tried to jump in and second Lanny but failed to grasp the understanding that had passed between the old man and Lanny.

"Hopefully, you'll let me see more of your *gifts* one day," Lanny said sincerely.

"Carmen," the old man's voice suddenly sharper, "you can bring—ah, Lanny is it?

"Yes sir, Lanny." And Lanny shot a big smile in Carmen's direction.

"*Si*, bring Lanny over anytime. I would be happy to show him some more of my work."

Carmen gave Lanny an annoyed look. Yolanda put her arm around Manuel and gave him a squeeze and glanced at Lanny.

116

"I told you you would meet a real *Santero* tonight and you've met the best."

"All right, all right," the old man protested. Too much praise can be unlucky, right, *'hita?*

"Not if it's the truth, Mr. Villafuerte," John gushed.

"Ay, Carmen," the old man wheezed through a laugh, "where did you get these two gringos? I like them a lot. Especially Mr. Lanny there."

The two men exchanged a quick look and Lanny understood that Manuel was showing Carmen that he had sized up Lanny and he was giving his approval. Carmen's annoyed look deepened.

"Well," the old man said at last seeing that Carmen was at a loss for words, "you kids go on and get something to eat. Mother's busy in the kitchen. I think I'll head off to bed."

Carmen gave Manuel a hug and a kiss. "'Night, Daddy."

The old man shuffled off down a hallway past the painted portraits, the daguerreotypes, and the black and white photos of his ancestors, becoming, as Lanny watched, a ghost-like figure of a man as he receded into the darkness of the hall.

"Carmen," Lanny began boldly, "I would be delighted if you would show me around your house and tell me about its history."

"Yeah," Yolanda agreed, while Carmen quickly frowned at her. "Why don't you show Lanny around?" Yolanda continued, taking John by the arm. "John and I will go to the kitchen and keep your mom company. Maybe she can show John how to make corn tortillas for me."

Yolanda ushered John off past the huge coat of arms and under an arched doorway leading off to the kitchen.

Carmen took a sharp-eyed look at the patient smile on Lanny's face and she whirled around and headed up the staircase, her hand grasping forcefully at the black wrought-iron handrail.

"Well, come on," Carmen said over her shoulder. "We might as well begin upstairs." And she flung her liquid black hair over her shoulder.

"As you wish." Again, speaking patiently.

Carmen turned to look back at Lanny and sighed angrily.

"Well, come on. Let's get this over with."

Indeed, Lanny thought as he followed her slowly, not matching her agitated pace. He looked up at her taut shoulders, hair bouncing in anger, and her rigid stride.

I wouldn't be surprised if she slapped me, Lanny thought. *Boy, I would hate to be the dog around this house tonight.*

At the top of the stairs Carmen waited for him and looked around quickly over the balcony to see if anyone was around. Her eyes flashed.

"How dare you!"

"I didn't and I don't dare anything," Lanny said calmly.

"I'm not just some hostess that needs to show you around!"

Carmen whirled around and walked down the hallway towards the door of her bedroom/workout room and flung it open.

Lanny continued his measured pace behind her, a slight smile of fate pulling at the corners of his mouth.

"You are angry," Lanny began.

Carmen could feel her neck getting hot and knew her face had a slight flush to it and that made her shake her head, angry that she couldn't hide it.

"Oh, angry am I?"

Lanny noticed again the cock of her head.

"Angry?" A curt laugh broke from her lips. "Angry is too strong a word. You annoy me. Simple as that."

Again speaking patiently. "I can't help the way you feel."

Carmen crossed her arms while one agitated wrinkle spread across her forehead. Lanny found himself fascinated as he watched its path and thought it was one of the most beautiful things he had ever seen.

"I can't tell if you're just being a gringo, being provocative, or if you're just stupid. You could tell my father is clearly in failing health, that he is ill. Where do you get off telling him that great cross was his last after I had told him, encouraged him, that there were plenty more crosses to come from him? He *will* be well soon."

Lanny dismissed Carmen's attack with a casual, masculine shrug of his shoulders.

Look at that, Carmen thought to herself as she shifted her weight, putting her hands on her hips. *He is so cocky and sure of himself. Gringos. Wasn't Andrew the same way?*

"I told him the truth and he knew it. You could see he appreciated that."

Yeah, right! Carmen rolled her eyes.

Lanny shrugged but continued. "Your father was glad to have someone acknowledge what he had been carrying around inside him. Simple as that," Lanny finished, taking on Carmen's tone.

"That's ridiculous," Carmen spat out, barely containing her contempt. "What the hell do you know? I know my father and he—"

Lanny stepped up to Carmen and looked down at her.

"You don't get it do you?" Lanny said, cutting her off, his voice rising though full of sadness. His blue eyes searched her face for a hint of understanding.

"Don't talk down to me," Carmen replied quickly as she threw back her hair. "Who in the hell asked you to feel sorry for me? I'll tell you what I—"

"Your father isn't just ill. He is dying."

"He's not dying!"

And Carmen let out a scoff of anger and frustration. She lifted her hand and started to slap Lanny. With a quickness that surprised Carmen, Lanny reached up and caught her forearm, his face calm, eyes full of compassion.

"He's dying and he knows it. He knew that cross would be his last effort, his last gift, and he wants those around him that he loves to recognize that and to let him know it's all right. That's his secret truth."

"You're crazy," Carmen almost hissed. "How do you know *his* truth?

Flatly. "It's the truth. Go and ask him."

"How can you come into my house and say such things. Oh, you presume...you presume way too much. I think you're—"

Lanny reached up with his hand and cupped Carmen's chin, and in one fluid, casual motion, he leaned down and kissed her full on the lips. The moment froze them together like a statue. Carmen felt the involuntary relaxing of her jaw. Lanny let go of her chin and Carmen put a hand to her lips as if to see if they were still on her mouth, while her black eyes gathered with fury.

"Oh, you are crazy as hell," she whispered, stifling her rage. "Now, keep your hands down while I give you the slap you deserve."   Lanny sensed Carmen gathering the muscles in her arm. He could feel fate passing through him and he could offer nothing but honesty.

"I hope you do…"
The moment tensed.

Lanny shrugged. "Go ahead if it will make you feel better. But I am not sorry that I took the kiss I wanted."

"Unable to stop it, the question shot out of her: "The kiss YOU wanted!?" Carmen rocked on her heels as if she had just received a blow.

Again that masculine shrug. "All right, the kiss that *you* wanted."

Carmen still felt back on her heels. "What?!"
Lanny took a quick look around and noticed the trail of clothes: bra, panties, socks… Carmen followed his gaze and remembered that she decided to just leave the clothes where she had discarded them. A quick look of anguish came over her face as she regretted opening her bedroom door. Lanny looked back to her calmly, his clear blue eyes looking deeply into hers.
That damn look, she thought: in the yoga room, the eyes above the luminaria floating in the embers and smoke.

"I don't know who you think you are but you're way out of line.

I—"

"Look, just be glad that I didn't take all…all that was offered."

Carmen's look of shock told Lanny what he already knew. She slowly stepped back from him, her hand coming up to cover her lips as if she didn't want them to betray her.

"I don't think I should stay for dinner," Lanny began. "Maybe when you are willing to be a little more polite to me, perhaps then. Maybe. Don't worry, I'll see myself out."

With that Lanny turned around and left, the feel of her lips still burning on his.

*Teaching tennis is not about telling people what to do or just showing them what to do, or running their asses off and then charging them fifty bucks because a "lesson" had just taken place. Teaching tennis is only helping people do what **they** can and technique can never be an end, only a means; and style should never dominate technique. Technique should never be dogma. It exists to serve the individual, not the other way around. There will always be an inherent tension between technique and style. The wise teacher has the ability to find the right balance between the two. Each person's particular physical and mental tendencies, the way each of their bodies wants to play, are the foundation on which to build a tennis style. But don't believe the mistaken notion that style equals freedom on the court. True freedom on the court can only be expressed from a foundation of technique. Only through the discipline of technique can you truly be free, no matter what skilled endeavor in which you are involved.*
And remember, freedom on the court, as in life, is only meaningful if it is limited by shrewd choices. So, the only two relevant questions the teacher has when beginning a student's training are: How much style? How much technique?
—Lanny Bedford, "The Long Hard Court"

What the hell have I gotten myself into? Lanny asked himself as a statement rather than as a question, as he watched his Men's 3.0 USTA team warm-up.

Spring had been trying to arrive in Santa Fe but the chill of winter could still be felt in the morning and at sunset. Four days ago snow had dusted the blossoming purple asters that lined the small walkway outside Lanny's door. The tops of the Sangre de Cristo *Mountains* were still covered with a wintery white blanket. The high desert air felt cool against his skin. Only his lips remained warm by the memory of *that kiss* and at times grew hot when he dreamed of Carmen's lips on his. Fate had provided him with courage that night and it had seemed so easy...so right. But, as the saying goes, fate is fickle and it didn't guide him anymore. *That kiss* changed everything, relinquishing the grip he had on his fateful courage. Walking home that night from Carmen's, past the burned-out *farolitos* and the smoldering luminarios on his way up Canyon Road, he pushed his hands deep into his pockets and hunched his shoulders against the cold. The street was deserted. The buoyancy of Christmas caroling and high spirits had retreated from the street with, it seemed to him, a finality as sure as the drop of a stage curtain.

That night he had been willing to accept anything that could have happened. *And that with a shrug!* But after tasting her lips and feeling the brief moment where their bodies had ached for a heated embrace, he knew. He knew with a pain that comes from sweet sadness that he could not now accept everything. That night had opened his heart, not just to the wind of the high mesa that blew right through the fate of the moment, but to the look of her, the feel of her, the potential feel of her all over his body, and yes, to the gut-wrenching thought of her rejection. He didn't feel destiny coursing through his veins but the sick spread of vulnerability. He knew that one look of disapproval from her would crush him. *Why?*

There's no way around it, he thought to himself as he poked away an errant ball with his racquet. *I'm scared.* He searched for the reasons why he felt he could lose everything if Carmen shot an annoyed glance at him. *Everything? Man...God help me. I couldn't take that look from her. Oh, damn, damn!*

For over two months Lanny had started every day with the admonition that he would go up to Carmen at the club and casually ask about her as if *The Kiss* had never happened and that the feelings he had for her that burned around in his heart like a fiery meteor were of no consequence. But upon seeing her come his way he would lose his nerve and duck down a hallway or, as it had happened a few times: retreat quickly into a utility closet while he swore at himself.

Fiercely, he tore his mind away from these thoughts and sought the refuge of the court, the reality between the lines. But the reality he saw before him made him crack a tight smile.

Man, look at those strokes. That's painful, Lanny told himself. *And the footwork...What footwork? They're not going to like what I have to say. So much for having fun. Well, they agreed to the conditions. But, did I really agree? Boy, I bet my old man would sure have a laugh if he knew what I was doing: going from the good chance of being a world-class player to teaching advanced beginners. But I had to get back to the court and if it's this way, so be it...Man, these guys aren't going to like what I have to say.*

And he remembered his father telling him that having fun on the tennis court is probably the most overrated concept to apply to tennis.

"Tennis is about delayed gratification," Paul Bedford would say as if to reveal the obvious, adding that "after the match, (after you had won), you can say you had fun. But you don't have fun during a match. All you have is concentration. You can't always have fun because that makes fun meaningless. Besides, if all you want to do is have fun, you'll never be a great tennis player, and being a great player means you never think you're great enough. What the hell does being great have to do with always having fun?"

Yeah, dad, you may be right, but this is a little different, Lanny thought to himself as he watched Jason clowning around at the net, using his racquet like a sword.

The Captain, Carl Holmes, had introduced the whole team to Lanny.

"We've got seven guys so far and one other singles player who's on the fence about playing with us. Hopefully he can be persuaded. I've set up a match between him and Pete here. So guys this is our coach, Lanny Bedford. We'll just call him 'Coach.' OK with you, Coach?"

Lanny nodded. "That'll be all right as long as none of you attaches an expletive to it."

The men chuckled.

"So, this is our team—that is, so far," Carl continued. "Raise your hand guys when I call your name and since we've all got nicknames for each other, I'll include that as well so Coach knows all the names. Paul Bodin. Surprise, we also call him

'Cajun'. Alex Cole. We like to call him Buddha because his droopy Fu Manchu and fat cheeks makes him look like a Buddha."

"And because on the court I'm so serene. Nothing bothers me."

"Yeah," Rocky blurted out, "that'll be the day."

"And that's Jason Rockington. We call him Rocky for short. Here's Pete F—"

"Pretty Boy Fuentes," Rocky broke in and gushed in a breathy voice. "Boy, I just love to say his name."

Pete gave Rocky a shove from behind.

"All right, guys," Carl continued, "And here is Jared Hightower. We all call him Junior."

"Yeah," Jared complained, "just like my Dad calls me. But I think I'm getting to old for it. Hell," he pouted, "I'm twenty four now."

"I told you boy," Bodin drawled with affection in his voice, "get used to it. You'll always be a junior because your old man is named Jared and he came first."

"Bummer," Junior spat out.

"That's all right, kid," Alex soothed, "when you can beat your old man at tennis then you'll stop being a Jr."

"That'll be never," Junior said dejectedly. "He's like the best player at the club, isn't he?"

All the men nodded their heads sadly showing sympathy.

"And here's Tom Tolson who we call 'Bottom Line.' The best CPA in town. He's a little high strung for being quiet as a mouse, but he kind of grows on you, don't you Tom?"

Embarrassed and self-conscious, Tom muttered something no one could hear.

"So, that's it," Carl said as he took off his hat and wiped his forehead. "The team."

Lanny squinted his eyes as the lowering sun's rays hit his face. "Carl, you know we'll have to get another guy just so we don't have to forfeit a match. Surely there are plenty of members in this club who would—"

"Tell him the truth, Carl," Rocky barked out.

"Well, ah," Carl began though his voice trailed off, "well, there are, but…"

Rocky jumped in again with his deep raspy voice: "Nobody wanted to play with us, right, Carl? Isn't that it? Because everybody you asked thought they were better than 3.0 and didn't want to play with a bunch of pushers and hackers, right?"

Carl looked at Lanny apologetically. "Well, that is just about right. Yep, that's right."

"Fuck 'em!" Tom Tolson blurted out and all the men paused, looking at each other as if to question what they had just heard because all the men knew that Tolson hardly ever said a word, let alone a harsh, nasty one. They all busted out laughing, with Rocky's wheezy laugh rising above the scattered guffaws.

Carl had to admit to Lanny, who was smiling: "Old Bottom Line's a bad-ass when he wants to be. You'll see."

Lanny watched the men laugh and poke at each other. Alex tried to give Tolson a chest bump and nearly knocked the diminutive man over.

The men scattered out onto the court and started hitting balls.

Someone will drop out, maybe two, Lanny predicted. *I wonder who it'll be. I wouldn't be surprised if the whole team falls apart. They're not really happy playing 3.0. They all think they're 3.5's. Yeah, their pride was hurt, all right. They're still steaming.*

"Hey, Coach! Did you see that big forehand?! Huh!? Huh!?" Jason Rockington yelled at Lanny in his good-natured way. "3.0, my ass. Nobody has ever seen a forehand like that at 3.0!" Jason thundered.

"Hey, Rocky, what good is that forehand if you can only make one out of ten?" Carl quipped.

"Come on, Skipper," Rocky feigned hurt, "you're supposed to keep my confidence up. That's no way for a captain to talk to one of his teammates."

"The Captain's not here to hold hands," Paul Bodin chimed in with his Cajun accent.

"Yeah," Alex Cole grunted in agreement as he tried to hit a serve into the deuce side. The serve went wildly out and almost hit Pete Fuentes who was standing over in the ad side. Pete quickly ducked out of the way with a startled shout.

"We always want the truth from our Captain," Alex said with conviction. "Yo! Sorry, Pete!"

"Everybody come on over here," Lanny gestured with his arms, his voice loud enough to get the men's attention. "Alex is right to want the truth from Captain Holmes and I suppose that's why you all agreed to have me coach you. The truth…That's always a good place to start on the court. You might get away with lying off the court but tennis always, and I mean always, punishes you for lying on the court. I am going to try to help you guys become competitive 3.0 players. You are not 3.5 players. I want you all to let go of that lie now."

Lanny saw Rocky shuffle his feet and could see a frown of stubbornness start to form on his face. Rocky was getting ready to say something but a sharp look from Carl persuaded him not to.

Lanny continued. "Because none of you have ever played competitive tennis I can assure you that if this team were to play in the 3.5 league you guys would not win one match and your scores would show a bunch of bagels and breadsticks for your efforts. I say we earn our way up the ladder, learn how to play, learn how to deal with pressure and our nerves and, most importantly, learn how to play with a partner."

"Nerves? Alex piped up, while he scratched at his potbelly. "What the hell, Coach, we're just playing tennis. It's just a game."

The men nodded and murmured to one another.

Lanny couldn't suppress a knowing chuckle.

"You may think it is. But that is another lie I want you guys to let go of. And I promise, if we get through this season together and go to the end you all will understand why that is a lie, and I will have done my job. And, as for nerves, just remember, it's hard to hit a second serve with both hands around your throat. And many of you, if not all of you, will have a go at that."

"What, me, choke?" Rocky blustered. "I thrive on pressure."

All at once the men laughed and mocked Rocky.

"We'll see," Lanny nodded and gave Rocky a cool, knowing smile that made the big man wipe off that look of bravado he had on his face.

"I know all you guys were looking forward to coming out and hitting some balls, playing some points. But I can tell from watching you guys hit that you aren't ready for that."

Looks of puzzlement, a few muttered questions, and some sarcastic laughter passed through the men.

"Coach," Alex cleared his throat. "Isn't tennis about hitting the ball? I mean, how can we play without hitting the ball?"

"Today," Lanny began, pulling on the bottom of his goatee, "like any other day we spend together, is going to be about learning, not playing."

"But Coach," Carl said, puzzled, "don't we have to hit the ball?"

Lanny paused, and he felt like a conduit for old Professor Burns whom he could feel speaking through him.

"Let me put it this way: today, even though we won't be hitting balls...we will be."

Again the mystified looks.

"Now, let's get started. To me, playing good tennis means one thing only: that you're playing from a foundation of good footwork. Your footwork will take you as far as you want to go in tennis. When you guys were hitting with each other, I didn't see any footwork. None."

"Are you suggesting that I'm fat and slow," Rocky tried to sound hurt.

Bodin cut in with his sardonic drawl. "He is and you are."

All the men laughed and agreed with Bodin.

"Maybe your teammates are," Lanny said through a smile, "but I'm suggesting that you have bad footwork because, number one, you aren't aware of your feet, and, number two, you don't know how to move your feet correctly."

"So, I'm not fat and slow?"

"Well," and Lanny took his time, "sorry, you are fat, but you don't have to be slow."

Rocky's smile was guarded. "There is hope then?"

"For everybody. Now, let's get started. Line up in two lines across the court with your racquets. By the time we finish you all will be split-steppin', cross-steppin', side-shufflin' masters. The key to hitting the ball well is balance, and balance can only come from good footwork. If your life is in balance you're living well; if you're balanced on the court you'll be playing well. It's that simple. Now, to become aware of your feet, close your eyes. Now, with your eyes closed, side-shuffle two steps to your right and then two shuffle steps to your left. Feel what your feet are doing. No, Alex, don't look at your feet. Keep your eyes closed so you can feel what your feet are doing. Now, take one step forward and then hop lightly onto the balls of your feet. Try to stay balanced on your toes for more than a moment. Step back and then forward again into your split-step, which is the same thing as coming to a jump-stop. Now you are balanced to go anywhere you need to: left, right, out-of-the-way. The split-step is a launching pad for you to go to the ball. The split-step is fundamental to all tennis movement. Without it, chances are you will seem to be fat and slow."

"Hey," Rocky gushed, "you mean instead of losing weight I could just split-step and be light on my feet and I wouldn't have to give up on the four meals a day?"

"That's correct."

"Wow, this split-step is for me, all the way to the buffet."

"And now you're going to come into your split-step and then cross-step to your right…and do it again and cross-step to your left. This is the basic footwork for your volley. All right, this the footwork we are going to work on today and we've got an hour and a half. Okay, and eyes closed. Here we go."

"Boy," Rocky couldn't help himself, "the next time officer Rael stops me and makes me do the roadside drunk test I'll pass with flying colors."

Oh, how I love being the underdog. The "pusher" is always the underdog. It's just a defensive game, people say derisively. Ha! My opponents don't realize how much ferocity and aggression lies behind my pushing. When you get beat by me, it's not just that I have defeated you. I have punished you. Having winners pounded past you is acceptable, but to have gotten a seemingly sure racquet on every one of my shots, every one of my pushes, and yet to have hit so many unforced errors, so many awkward shots, so many frustrating shots—now that is punishment.

—At The Public Courts: Conversations with the Professor, alias "The Pusher"

Lanny smiled grimly as he watched Herman Tsosie play. He noted the look in Herman's eyes: that kind of glazed over light of pure ferocity that a bulldog has when biting down on a bone. *Man, what a backboard,* Lanny thought. *A grunt and a push, a grunt and a push. That's how it'll go the whole match. Pretty Boy Fuentes doesn't know what pain he's in for.*

"Well, Skipper, I think we've got our other singles player," Lanny said to Carl Holmes, who was standing next to him.

Carl looked incredulous. "Are you serious, coach? I mean, look at the way he hits the ball. He couldn't—

At that moment a ball slammed into the fence just above their heads and they heard Pete Fuentes utter a vehement curse. Only three games had gone by and the supremely fit Fuentes was sweating profusely in the dry, high desert air. He was clearly agitated and was talking to himself. Tsosie nonchalantly tossed his glistening black ponytail over his shoulder, his Navajo features inscrutable. He clearly looked girded for battle. Every joint was strapped down, both knees sheathed in elastic braces, the right elbow and wrist wrapped in tight Velcro. His left ankle bulged from some sort of bulky leather support and every other finger was taped up. Tsosie came from a family of Navajo jewelers who owned a store downtown. In the southwest jewelry business he was known for his striking and creative style, reinterpreting the classic Navajo settings. People from all over the states came to buy his turquoise jewelry. But his tennis style showed none of the creativity of his craft. Instead it revealed an attention to regularity and an expression of regimented action that would warm any Swiss watchmaker's heart.

"Who is that guy?" Carl wondered as he watched Tsosie, his dark Indian skin resembling a well-oiled machine. Carl took off his sunglasses and cleaned them on his shirt, as if something clouded—no, as if something disturbed his view. *Damn, every one of his strokes look the same. Ugly and the same.*

Lanny looked sideways at Carl and read his mind. "Ugly, eh?"

"What?" Carl tried to sound surprised, shifting his weight from one foot to the other. "Oh, you mean the match. Well, Yeah."

"No, I mean Herman's game. The way he hits the ball. You think it's ugly, don't you? Look at him scuttle around the court like he has a frying pan in his hand and not a racquet. The continual cock and push," Lanny said as he watched the action in front of him through the fence.

"I'm not saying I have the greatest looking game," Carl said quickly, "but boy oh boy, I hope I don't look like that when I hit the ball. Anyway, Fuentes will take him down. He's too athletic; he's in great shape, and his strokes are better."

Lanny turned and looked at Carl with a you-don't-get-it expression and Carl tried to shrug him off. *He can't be serious about this Indian guy, can he?* Carl asked himself.

"You know how Pretty Boy likes to hit the ball hard. He always misses a few, like that one," Carl said, motioning towards the court.

Lanny nodded without conviction. "Well, you watch, Skipper, there will be a lot more like that one."

Carl's face turned serious and his brow knotted. "You think it'll be a short match?" Carl asked as he picked at his nose.

Experience made Lanny shake his head. "No, that's not the way Herman plays. It'll be three sets. I understand Herman's game." And again Lanny smiled grimly. "Herman doesn't just want to beat Pretty Boy, he wants to punish him. Be ready to give some words of encouragement to Pete when it's over. He may want to quit tennis." Lanny looked off into the distance and his eyes turned inward. "I know. I've been there."

Tsosie reminded Lanny of "The Pusher," old professor Burns.

One late afternoon at Lincoln Park in Santa Monica, while the leaves on the palm trees fluttered in the slight, off shore breeze, Lanny furiously pounded balls against the practice wall. He caught himself grunting with each stroke and then he would stop, reminding himself that only Jimmy Connors could grunt. His father had taken him to see the UCLA freshman phenom and young Lanny, at a little over twelve years of age, had been mesmerized—while others were mostly shocked—at Connors' on-court ferocity.

Lanny noticed that a sloped-shouldered, gray-haired man was watching him from behind thick lenses. The man continued to watch Lanny with a quiet intensity. Finally, Lanny stopped as if the man had called to him. They stared at each other for a moment and Lanny thought how the man didn't look like a tennis player, with his stooped frame and overly long Bermuda shorts that touched his bandy knees.

Suddenly, (it seemed suddenly to Lanny), a deep, cultured, resonant voice sounded, and for a brief moment Lanny thought the voice was coming from somewhere else, not from the frail man in front of him.

"I see you are determined to beat the wall," the man said, a slight smile on his tight lips. "My name is Burns, everyone calls me Professor Burns. And you, my big-hitting young man?"

Lanny walked over and carefully introduced himself, at the same time studying the old academic in front of him.

Who is this beginner? Lanny thought to himself. *I hope he doesn't ask me to play. Oh, boy, look at the poor old guy.*

If the old bugger asked, Lanny knew he would have to hit with him because his father had told him to always hit with someone who asks you, because there were times when someone much better than you might agree to hit a few balls.

My, look at the swagger in his walk, Professor Burns noticed as Lanny walked up to him. *Sure enough, he's a cocky little one. Good strokes. No question about that. Let's see if I can give him a surprise. I'll give him my ugly Jack Kramer imitation. He'll be overconfident. They always are.*

If he does ask me to hit, Lanny thought coyly, *I'll make it quick, because I've got to go home and do my homework. That'll get him. After all, he's a professor and all of that.*

"Shall we hit a few balls together?" the deep voice asked.

An hour later, as Lanny now remembered fondly, "The Pusher" had pushed and sliced him all over the court, leaving him sweating and blowing hard, frustrated almost to the point of tears, while Professor Burns with his Ichabod Crane body hadn't even broken a sweat. Mercifully, the match ended quickly.

"I am sorry if you are frustrated," the deep voice said in a matter-of-fact tone as they shook hands at the net. "Are you?"

"Why should I be?" Lanny blurted out, unsuccessfully hiding his feelings, his face hot, his eyes lowered for fear of what they would reveal.

"I see."

The Professor straightened his strings with his nicotine-stained fingers. "You *were* frustrated," the Professor said.

Pause. Lanny thumped his racquet face against the heel of his tennis shoe. Thump. Thump. Thump.

"So what? It's no big deal."

"If you can't master your frustration on the court," the deep voice intoned, "you won't be a great player."

"Hey, I was just hitting with you, you know?" Lanny said quickly, disdain in his child's voice. "I was...doing you a favor. My dad told me that I had to.

"I see." The Professor said, nodding, then he turned his dark glasses at Lanny and said: "Whom the Gods would destroy, they first make mad."

"What's that mean?" Lanny finally asked, pouting.

"Simply put: a mad player is a bad player."

"So?" Lanny continued, with an air of indifference in his voice.

"Well, that's for you to answer, not me," the Professor said smoothly, while he took off his sunglasses and looked Lanny directly in the eye.

Lanny broke away from the Professor's intense gaze and turned his head and tried to fight off the sentence that surged to his lips. Finally, he couldn't hold it back and turned back to the professor who looked at him as if he knew what Lanny was about to say.

"I am sorry, but you really don't…"

"Please, my dear boy. You can be frank with me. I won't crumble," the Professor said with a twinkle in his eye.

"You…ah, you really don't play tennis," Lanny said at last.

"Oh, that's it." And the Professor allowed himself a deep chuckle. "I thought so. So, I am not a tennis player? Is that what you in your youthful wisdom have concluded?"

"But you're not," Lanny insisted.

"Who just kicked whose behind?" the professor said, an edge creeping into his deep voice.

Lanny fidgeted. Thump. Thump. Thump.

"So. It doesn't matter."

"If we were to go out there and play again, could you beat me?" the Professor asked with a hint of sarcasm.

"Like I said," Lanny began, frustrated, "it doesn't matter."

"Because?" The professor prodded, in the same tone he used when engaging a student of his.

Silence. Thump. Thump. Thump.

"Because," the Professor answered, "because you don't respect me. Don't you want to beat me? Aren't you angry that I kicked your butt so easily? Well!?" Burns asked loudly.

I've got him squirming on the hook now, Burns thought, hoping that the lesson would go as planned.

"Yes, I am mad," Lanny said, his face squinted in anger and he squeezed his racquet hand until his knuckles turned white.

"You want to beat me?" the Professor continued in his Socratic line of questioning.

"Yes," Lanny said flatly.

"Then respect me!" the Professor barked slamming his racquet head on the net cord for emphasis. "Let me tell you something, young man: You will find my type of game at every level of tennis. If you want to beat me, than had you better respect me. It's a weakness not to respect your opponent. Don't ever forget that. And never forget," Burns dropped his stern tone, "that you are going to be a great player."

Lanny's rightly chastened expression turned to astonishment. "Do you really mean it?" Lanny asked hopefully.

Burns' tight lips smiled. "I certainly do. But you'll have to beat me first."

"Give me some time, Professor," Lanny said, smiling back at Burns.

"So," the professor began rhetorically, "you wish to be a strong and confident player?"

Lanny nodded his head emphatically.

Good, Burns thought to himself, *the lesson went better than I thought. The kid has great promise. So it begins.*

"It all begins with respect, son…for yourself and your opponent. Respect is the foundation of a champion's game. Don't forget it. It's also the basis of being a good and useful human being. You'll see."

Thus had their friendship started. Old Burns loved to play out a point and then stop and analyze it. And Lanny couldn't help but listen to that commanding, deep voice. But now, after all of these years, it pained him to realize that he had failed old Professor Burns, whom he knew had died about ten years ago.

What would the old boy say to me now? Lanny asked himself a sense of loss echoing off the walls of his question.

Fuentes was now making faces at Tsosie's shots and snorting derisively when Tsosie pushed another ball back in play, taking the pace off the ball.

The third set went quickly, 6-1 for Tsosie. Fuentes was so pissed that he barely shook hands with Herman. He angrily tossed his racquet into his bag.

Carl looked at Lanny. "Boy, you sure called that one. I never would have thought Herman stood a chance.

135

"Like I said, I've seen it before and have experienced it. It's brutal," Lanny said remembering all too well the lesson Professor Burns had given him that balmy day when he had felt so sure and arrogant about himself.

"Tough match," Carl said in sympathy to Pete as he came onto the court.

"Sorry," Pete began as he noticed Lanny standing next to Carl, and Lanny thought to himself:
Now here come the excuses.

"Sorry coach, I didn't show you much today. I played like shit. I hurt my back the other day working out and I just couldn't get loose...
Here comes another one.

"Also, I've been thinking about changing my racquet. It doesn't feel right anymore."

"I know Pete could have played a lot better today," Herman said graciously.

Lanny rubbed his nose with his forefinger and thumb and then stroked his goatee. Lanny knew what he had to say to Pete. *Let's see how this goes.*

"Herman, you played really well today," Lanny said. "I was very impressed. Yep, he played well, didn't he, Pete?"

"Yeah," Pete replied with a slight undertone of sarcasm, "if you say so."

"My game is, well, unusual," Herman said, almost apologizing but Lanny could tell he was secretly relishing Pete's excuses. "People can have a tough time with my game, especially if they haven't played me before."

"I'll say," Pete snorted in a mocking way that was obvious to everyone and he smoothed back his full head of salt and pepper hair. Herman's inscrutable expression didn't change as he slowly took off all his wraps and supports, like a knight peeling off his armor.

"Yeah, but I still think Herman played really well, don't you Pete?" Lanny asked pointedly, thinking: *I've got to get him off his high horse.*

"He sure had his way with me," Pete said his tone still not showing respect for Herman.

"He had his way with you because he is a better player than you are. An old hacker who taught me a lot about the game of tennis told me that the scoreboard is not for pictures, just numbers. If you and Herman played five more times the score would be the same. Herman will remain a better player if you keep thinking it doesn't matter if he wins because everyone knows you have better, technical-looking strokes and an orthodox serve."

Pete's eyes widened with the realization that Lanny had been reading his mind. He shot a look at Carl, who slowly nodded his head.

"You should thank Herman," Lanny said looking directly into Pete's eyes, "for providing you with an excellent chance to improve your game, because you're never any good until you beat someone better than you." And then Lanny turned to look at Carl, prompting him while Pete absorbed the truth of what Lanny had said to him.

Carl said, "Herman, the guys would love for you to play with us and be our number one singles player. What do you think?"

Herman was clearly pleased by Carl's offer but he hesitated, being naturally self-effacing.

"I appreciate that Carl, I really do. But I don't know about playing in a real league. I beat a lot of people around here but when we play those teams from Albuquerque—with my game—I don't think I could stand up well against those guys."

"Don't worry about your game, Herman. You'll be fine, believe me," Lanny persuaded.

"Yeah, don't worry about your game," Pete spoke up and Lanny and Carl looked at one another in surprise. "I think your game is fine. You really kicked my butt and I've got to hand it to ya. I want to ask you personally to be on the team because I need someone to push me and as today demonstrated, you certainly can. How about it?" And Pete offered his hand to Herman, who took it and shook it firmly saying: "How can I refuse?"

"Great," Carl gushed. "That's great. Now we have our two singles players." And he then looked at Lanny. "What do you say, Coach, are you going to let us start hitting balls and playing? I mean, we've had four practices and have yet to hit one ball. The guys are getting restless, really restless," Carl said, trying to contain the frustration in his voice. "The guys tell me that they're even dreaming about their footwork. They're grumbling, I'll tell you that."

Lanny turned to Carl, his forefinger and thumb brushing at his nose.   "Getting a little mad, are they?"

"Guess you could say that."

"Anybody talk about quitting, Captain Holmes?" Lanny asked calmly.

"No!" They all said defiantly.

Remember the deal, if one quits then we're finished. In team tennis unity is the highest value. The team, the team…the team. In the beginning and in the end: the team. Right, captain Holmes?"

"I'm with you, Coach."

"When you're out there playing at 3-doubles and your match is the deciding match, you want that team concept to be ingrained. I want the guys to *want* to fight for the team, for their teammates. Fighting for your brothers is a higher motivation then just for yourself. This is team tennis. We win together, we lose together. No one person can be given the whole credit for a win or a loss. The first time I hear that from someone, the team is finished and I'm done."

"I remember your conditions, coach."

"Do the guys?"

"I hope so."

"Good," Lanny nodded, "that's really good. So, do you think the guys are ready to have at each other?"

"Man, are we ever!"

Pressure: it has all kinds of mothers during a match. What's to be done about it? Actually nothing. Accept the pressure, even welcome it and welcome it you must, for it shapes you as much as the raw wind does the highest and mightiest peak. And there's nothing the peak can do about the wind.
—At The Public Courts: Conversations with the Professor, alias "The Pusher"

An innocent walk last night to prepare, in his mind, for tomorrow's practice, ended up in front of Carmen's house. He looked across the antebellum stone bridge, the spring wind blowing dried out tumbleweeds around his legs, his hair whipping around his forehead like tattered shutters banging against an old abandoned adobe. He felt as if something within him would let go entirely, then the wind would sweep him up like a lifeless leaf and toss him into a whirlwind, and off he would go into the inky night as anonymously as any unrequited feeling. Soft lights emanated from the inset windows of the house, like slow smoke rising out of a kiva chimney.

God, he had thought to himself, *I was never a coward on the court, but this…Jesus… There's no way I'm going to knock on that gate.*

Lanny scoffed at his own temerity.

The sound of tennis balls being hit brought him out of his dark thoughts, bringing him back to the reality he preferred and relished. He watched for a while, his forefinger and thumb stroking his nose. Yes, his guys were practicing hard, playing hard, trying hard, but? but??? They were playing without a purpose, just hitting shots. They needed a…philosophy.
Yeah, that's right.

He remembered old Professor Burns asking him the question when he was twelve:

"Tell me, my boy, what's your philosophy of tennis? It's the most important question you'll ever ask yourself. No need to squirm. Yes, I know you are only twelve. No one is ever too young to consider philosophy. If you want to be and act like a man on the

139

court, you'd best have a philosophy. You don't always want to be a child playing at tennis, do you?"

Lanny remembered piping out a few "no, no, no's," in his child's voice.

"No, no, no, Jason," Lanny barked out in a deep voice. "What kind of shot was that?" as he strode out onto the court, the late afternoon sun laying long shadows across the hard surface.

Jason shuffled his feet and a puzzled look came over his face.

"I don't know, just a shot. I was trying to angle the ball off, to hit it away from Bodin there."

"That was the fifth time you've tried that shot. How many times have you made it?"

Jason began to look flustered. "I don't know. Maybe one or —"

"I'll tell you," Lanny broke in. "None. Not one."

"I'm just tryin' to hit it where nobody can get it, Coach," Rocky said plaintively.

"I know you are but let's look at the percentages; let's accept the fact that we're 3.0's; let's accept the fact that that short angle you were trying to hit is a damn tough shot. How many feet of court did Jason have to work with? Captain Holmes?"

"Not much," Carl said quickly." Not much."

"Not much is right," Lanny continued. "I'd say about fifteen feet, now, if you all are Jason, what's the easiest shot to hit?"

"Well, you all know me," Bodin began in his slow accent, "I'm gonna lob."

Lanny smiled and all the guys started laughing.

"We know old Bodin likes to lob, hell, he'd lob his serve if he could," Rocky said with a smirk. "But me, I like to stroke the ball so—"

"So," Lanny cut in. "Hit the damn ball down the middle."

"But, Coach," Rocky said in protest, "Bodin and Carl were standing right in front of me, I figured they could reach the ball if I hit it down the middle and I know they sure as hell couldn't reach that little angle ball."

"Look, don't be afraid to let your opponent try and hit the ball back. Believe me, if you hit that ball down the middle they're going to have a hell of time getting it back, if at all, and you are taking all their angle away by making them volley from the middle of the court. I guarantee you that if they do get a racquet on the middle ball you hit, nine times out of ten you will be able to get a racquet on the ball that comes back. The middle is always, almost always, open. If you are ever in doubt as to where to hit the ball, hit it down the middle. So, from now on, here's our doubles philosophy: we win by hitting the ball down the middle; we are going to beat people down the middle but, but we're not going to get beat down the middle; we serve down the middle, we volley down the middle, we return down the middle, hit our strokes down the middle—

"Lob down the middle," Bodin chimed in.

"Yes," Lanny smiled, "we lob down the middle too."

"But Coach," Alex scratched at his beer belly, "hitting those angle shots are cool. I see those 3.5 guys hit 'em all the time."

Lanny looked around at the men, taking his time so he had their full attention.

"Yeah, that may be, but you guys are 3.0's. 3.0's are 3.0's because they can't hit that shot consistently."

"But how are we going to get to be 3.5's if we don't try to hit that shot until we get it," Rocky said flatly, which drew a hard stare from Carl.

Lanny let a tight smile gather at the sides of his mouth.

"Do you guys want to win, or do you want to lose while pretending to be 3.5's? Are we agreed or not? Next week, when we play our first match, I don't want to see any of you try and hit a short angle unless your nose is on top of the net. Everything goes down the middle. Don't even worry about going up the line. Forget about it. Agreed?" And Lanny looked at each of the men.

"Of course we agree," Carl said first, "and we are ready for our first match, right guys?"

Affirmative replies all around.

"Piece of cake," Rocky said assuredly, "we're gonna have some fun and kick some butt. Right, Coach?"

Lanny nodded his head and picked at the ball fuzz on his racquet strings.

"My job is to help you guys win. That's why you're paying me the big bucks."

Laughter and snickers greeted Lanny's words.

"So," Lanny continued, "we are going to win by hitting the ball down the middle. The middle?"

Pause.

"The middle," Carl said his voice rising.

Lanny looked around.

"The middle?"

More voices but not enough: "The middle."

All eyes went to Rocky who hadn't said anything.

Lanny looked directly at Rocky. "The middle, Rocky?"

Always the ham, Rocky knew he had everybody hanging. Carl's mouth was twitching and Bodin silently prompted Rocky like a Cajun looking up from a sour glass of red wine.

Rocky suddenly raised his fist high. "The middle!!! The middle!!!"

All the men started raising their fists and shouting out:

"The middle! The middle!

Lanny's face and eyes shared their enthusiasm but his mind told him that this might be the last time they shared such an exaltation of team spirit.

They, he thought to himself, *have no idea what they're about to face. It ain't the game they think it will be. It could be brutal. Yep, it could easily be brutal with a capital B.*

The volley is the most beautiful thing in tennis. Mastering the volley brings you the closest to what is perfection in tennis. Requiring the most skill of all tennis shots, the volley is, at the same time, the most simple. And it is that simplicity that is elusive. Never forget that the ultimate goal of skill is simplicity. The correctly executed volley in all its sublime technique is as memorable as anything nature can regale the eye with."
—At the Public Courts: Conversations with the Professor, alias "The Pusher."

And it was brutal. No match lasted more than forty-five minutes, except for Herman's singles match that went for (no surprise, Lanny thought) two and a half hours, with Herman winning 7-5 in the third set. With Herman's mechanically awkward style coupled with his fierce need to prove himself because of it, and his jewelry craftsman's love of concentration, he was able to overcome a more skilled opponent.

And it was ugly. Lanny was still in shock at how many double faults his team had, literally double-faulting away game after game, not to mention the dozen or so outright whiffs that had made him usher up all the control he had to keep his face calm, expressionless, lest he dishearten the troops. Figuratively, they were bloody and beaten as they headed off the courts, their heads down as far as they could go, a look of defeat and disbelief in their lowered eyes.

Only Rocky was storming and blowing with anger and frustration. Lanny had always thought Rocky would be the one to quit first, and of course that would end the season according to the rules Lanny had set down.

"I don't think," Rocky thundered like a wounded bull, "that one of those bastards on that team was under sixty-five! Jesus, Mary, and Joseph!" Rocky erupted, "we got beat by a bunch of old grandpas!"

"Shoot me, somebody," moaned Pretty Boy Fuentes, running his fingers through his perfect hair. "I was serving to start the match and then—shit, who-the-hell-knows-what-happened—

143

and then it was over. Just like that." And he shook his head in shock.

"Well, our story isn't much better, eh, Bodin?" Carl had to admit, his voice quiet.

"Nope," Bodin replied lowly.

"I think we got beat 1 and 1, and it wasn't that close," Carl said dejectedly, taking off his hat and rubbing his forehead as if to erase the memory from his mind. "Damn, I couldn't move, I couldn't see the ball. I don't know what the hell was in my mind and I could never remember the damn score."

All the men nodded because they had shared the same experience.

"It was soooo weird," Jr. piped up. "I couldn't toss the ball on my serve. It wouldn't come out of my hand, and when it did—man, it was sailing all over the place. It made me dizzy just trying to watch it."

"I hate losing to a bunch of old fuckers," Tolson hissed out vehemently through clinched teeth. His thick glasses already made his eyes seem overly large and his outburst made them bulge out, ready to bust through his turtle-shell frames.

Lanny didn't say anything. He knew they weren't through. But he knew they were close. All they needed was for someone—

"I mean, if this is the way it's going to be—who needs this shit," Rocky said defiantly.

That's it, Lanny thought to himself. *They're finished.*

"I mean," Rocky continued on, his chin jutting out, "we practiced hard, came out here to play a game and what do you call that shit we just participated in?" he asked rhetorically.

"Shit," seconded Buddha, who pulled dejectedly on his Fu Manchu.

"That's right. Shit." Fuentes muttered.

"*Mon Dieu,* that was some sorry shit, sure enough," drawled Bodin while he scratched at the side of his face.

"It was tough out there today. Very tough for all of us, except Herman," Carl had to admit.

"Tough?!" Rocky snorted out sarcastically. "Tough, Carl? Maybe your 1 and 1 match was tough but old Alex and I got our asses kicked—hell it was worse than that. We were, and let's tell it like it was: we were just plain bitch-slapped and those old farts just smirked the whole time. I could have swore that one of our opponents had some diapers on under his tennis shorts. I mean, come on!" Rocky finished with disgust in his voice as he threw his racquet bag down on the ground.

"It's humiliating," Alex said, sighing through his disgust.

"I mean, who needs this shit," Rocky growled. "I don't. I mean, all those sorry-ass balls, the lobs, and the dinks. Remember that one grizzled bastard, what was his name?"

"Norton," Alex said as if remembering the name of a nightmare.

"Yeah, Norton, damn his ass, he lobbed every frickin' ball that came his way. I think he even lobbed his serve once. I mean, what kind of tennis is that?" Rocky spat out plaintively.

"One of the old dudes we were playing against was still using a wooden racquet. I couldn't believe it," Jr. said shaking his head.

"Oh, man, that's too much. A wooden racquet. Jesus," Alex continued in his bitter tone.

"I don't know about the rest of you but I'm done. I don't need this shit," Rocky said resolutely as he folded his arms across his chest.

Lanny, hands on his hips, took all of this in. The men stole looks at him. The silence tensed around them.

Carl spoke up, clearing his throat.

"Look, guys, it was just one match. Our first match. So, things didn't go our way."

Rocky scoffed and shuffled his feet.

Silence.

Finally Lanny lifted his chin, as if coming to a conclusion in his mind, and said: "Seems to me that those guys you played were…and are better then you. Simple as that. Disparage their game if you want to but they kicked your asses because they were better than you. Accept it. But I know that's tough to take when you like to think you're all 3.5's, huh, Rocky?"

Arms still folded, Rocky looked straight at Lanny.

"Look, I've played with the 3.5 guys at the club and I can pretty much hold my own, but with those codgers today, man, that was just shit and we all know it."

"Yeah, who needs it," two voices sounded together. Lanny thought it was Alex and Pete.

Lanny looked around, thinking that what he was about to say would be his last words to them. *Interesting experiment, I guess*, he sighed mentally to himself.

"Remember, I told you at the beginning that there was one lie that I wanted you guys to let go of and that was that tennis is just a game. Competitive tennis is not just a game. I guess you guys found that out today. I can understand if competition isn't what you guys really want to deal with or be challenged by. You probably have enough of that in your working lives. I understand and now you understand what I meant. An old man I once knew told me that competitive tennis is a crucible at any skill level."

Lanny studied the men around him and saw dejected faces, anger, and still shock. No need for this torture to go on any longer.

I'll pull the trigger for them. I'm sure they'll agree, Lanny decided.

"All right, guys. Hey, it was interesting. You all had a taste and found you didn't like it. You can go back to enjoying some social tennis back at the club and that's that."

Again Lanny looked around and saw that a silent consensus was gathering, agreeing with what Lanny said. Even Carl, Captain Holmes, Lanny noted, had a look of resignation on his face. Carl caught Lanny's eye and almost started to speak, an effort at exhortation that died on his lips like the last syllables of expiring faith.

That's it, then.

Lanny said: "I'll see you guys around the club."

Lanny walked through the men as they backed away to give him space to pass. He tried to look at every one of them in the eye. None raised their eyes to his except for Herman whose dark eyes said something about appreciation and Lanny nodded.

Again Carl started to say something but couldn't and finally said this as Lanny walked away: "Thanks for all your help, Coach."

Lanny just raised his arm but didn't turn around. The men watched him walk away for a moment.

A throat cleared as if summoning up the courage to speak.

"Hey guys," the soft-spoken Herman began, his dark Indian face inscrutable, full of thick shadows and sharp angles. He fingered his ponytail that hung down to one side of his chest. "I just wanted to say that I really appreciate having the chance to play on this team. I don't know what this is worth but I say we let the results of this battle today lie down for a while before we dissolve the team. You know we Indians are full of sayings. Again, for what it's worth, as one of my ancestors said: 'Don't make a group decision when the blood is still wet...' So I don't think we should make a decision until we have a chance next week to sit down, have some food and a sweat." Herman finished his sentence with a note of humility, and that tone raised a few dejected heads. Even Rocky had to look up, his mind weighing what Herman had said.

Seizing the moment, Carl jumped, realizing the idea was making the men reconsider, at least for the moment.

"Herman's right, guys. Let's think it over."

Pause.

"Well then," Carl continued quickly, "if nobody wants to quit now, we'll do as Herman has suggested—ah, Herman, I understand the food part but what did you mean about a sweat?"

*I don't know if my son will ever find **his** woman. He never had the love of his mother. And I am sure that is an unrelenting knowledge for him; a constant companion of pain. The more I tried to say how sorry I was about that, because I had had his mother's love, he would just smile that slow survivor's smile of his that shamed me and my tears, and pat me on the back—comforting me! Oh, I hope he finds or is found by the kind of love that was between his mother and me. Lanny, do you hear me? I wish it. I wish it so much...*

—Paul Bedford. "Notes to my son." A Personal Diary.

Lanny trudged up the mountainous trail. He slipped and then adjusted his feet as if he were shifting a heavy backpack to a better position. He paused. He carried nothing on his back but the irrepressible burden of despair. This morning, in the mirror his eyes had seemed defeated and he wondered why, especially lately, every time he looked at himself in the mirror he expected to see something different, (a different look) than the resigned one staring back at him. He had shaken his head and the look had vanished but not the white-hot memory of *that* look: Carmen's total rejection of him. Harsh words would have been far kinder. Only the eyes can be so cruel, so...final.

He shuddered before the mirror and for a moment squinted his eyes with the pained memory of it all. After the team had decided to take Herman's suggestion of "food and a sweat," Lanny had just nodded, saying "Just let me know what you decide," and had walked back up to the clubhouse, still thinking that the team was finished. As he turned the corner to make his way past the front desk, preoccupied with the team match and how he might have prepared them better, he almost plowed right into Carmen, who his imagination told him—had been waiting for him just for this moment. Startled, Lanny drew back, his voice gone. Carmen's momentary loss of poise—which she always hated— was quickly masked by a quick look of disdain and irritation. Soundless, he looked at her. Three quick beats went by like the sound of tolling bells that summoned townspeople to a noontime hanging. And then she blew by him, her look, like a body blow to the heart, made him step back to gain his balance. It had been quick and merciless.

He could still feel the vertigo in his heart as his love for Carmen reeled down, down into the void, burdened by all his fears and despair; when it hit bottom it would burst through his heart like a shooting star. It would burn bright with a red-hot intensity and then… extinguished itself with the velocity of its fall.

He shook his head again, this time to shake the sweat out of his eyes and to blot out that gut-wrenching memory. He wanted to make the mirror's image in his mind fade out as he hiked up the rocky, steep trail, pushing and punishing his legs until his thighs and calves burned. The trail snaked through switchbacks first up and then down into the small canyons behind St. John's College.

The sun began its slow descent, weakening the gusty breeze and throwing off its angled light that sharpened and deepened the colors and shadows around him. He paused for a moment and looked over the hills stretched out before him, hills covered with *chamisa*, creosote bush, and the mix of high desert *piñon* and juniper. Farther up he could see groves of aspens, their smooth, light bark clearly visible. The waning breeze that coursed down the mountains brought the sound of quaking aspen leaves. Off to the right, color on the hillside caught his eye. High Plains flowers sprouted from under low Coyote Willow trees and lay tucked away like jewels in swales: Lanceleaf, Coreopsis, purple asters, Firewheels. All along the cut out trail there were patches of Western Blue Flag, Black Foot Daisies, and clumps of cactus with bright, tightly pedaled flowers bursting from their wide prickly ends.

Damn, life is so tenacious, Lanny thought to himself. *It seems to take whatever chances it gets to be what it is.* Lanny paused on the heel of one foot, his forefoot poised above a lone stem of Blue Flax. *How vulnerable this flower is; how easily it could be crushed. How easily I was crushed. But what does it want? Nothing, I bet. It has no expectations, no hopes. Man, that's strength.*

Lanny stepped away from the flower and again he looked up and out across the Sangre de Cristo Mountains. He filled his chest with the fresh but thin air, sighed, and wondered where the wave that had swept him up in L.A. would take him now as he felt it gathered behind him, swelling with his despair and his funereal sadness. Yet another loss. Another ex? *No,* he thought, *Carmen couldn't be an ex. No, something worse. She was never mine and that's what makes it worse....Damn.*

For the most part, though, he had made peace with his past. He had returned to the courts and the muddy bottom of his river had stilled and lay dormant under the crystal flowing water. He had forgotten how much solace and refuge could be had by just being on the courts. It had become again his milieu, his natural environment. But he knew that once he finished his coaching commitment, the wave that Carmen caused to rise up behind him would take him somewhere else. His stomach grew tight every time he had to go up to the club for practice or when he thought she was watching him from the shaded workout windows as he hit some balls with John. Then, as he had turned to walk around that fateful corner by the front desk, he ran into that *look* and one was all he could bear.

Again he sighed to comfort himself. Only when his eyes let go of their stoicism, and tears began to break free one deep ache at a time, did he realize what the cost of this new loss would be.

A dart of movement caught his eye in the canyon below him. There was no mistaking that flash of jet-black hair that caught the late afternoon sunlight like a mirror's reflection. His heart leapt. *Carmen!!!*

She broke through a dense patch of piñon her strong strides gliding her along, the muscle tone in her long legs showing with each step.
An urge made him start to raise his hand but he swallowed her name before it could burst from his lips. He lowered his hand in defeat. And he heard old Professor Burns' voice in his head:

"When you lose because of a weakness it always costs you more than when you lose while being strong."

Lanny heard her melodious laugh and saw her turn her head to say something to someone who was behind her. A figure emerged from the piñon patch trying to catch up to her. *A man!* The man yelled a deep voiced epithet at her that Lanny couldn't make out. But the tone carried an easy familiarity. Carmen slipped on a steep part of the trail and fell backward. The man roughly caught her by the buttocks and pushed her back up with a bark of laughter. *She's with him!!!*

A single thought forged in his mind, its molten letters glowing red: I LOVE HER!

Lanny clenched his fists, gathered his voice in all its pain and passion and let it bellow down into the canyon.

"CARMEN!!! CARMEN!!! CARMEN!!!"

He saw Carmen stop. She shaded her eyes and looked up towards him. The man looked up as well. Lanny whispered to himself while his heart pounded in his chest. "Carmen, oh, Carmen."

Carmen paused a moment, said something to the man behind her and then turned and headed down the trail, the man following her.

Instinct made Lanny bolt down the hiking path. He recklessly skidded through the switchbacks. Startled cicadas buzzed from the dense piñon that lined the trail and dive-bombed him as he rushed by them. He had to get to her and tell her all that was in his heart. He didn't care if he made a scene. Who cares who that man is or what he is to her. Lanny knew what she meant to him and he was going to let her know.

"Carmen!"

Flying down the trail, with each footfall almost sliding out from under him, Lanny burst down into the floor of the canyon. Unable to stop his hurtling momentum, he overran the trail and flew into a thicket of piñon, sending the cicadas into a buzzing panic. The thicket broke his fall but tore scratches along his arms and bare legs. A blunt branch gashed his forehead just above his right eyebrow. He felt the blood leak down onto his eyebrow. Grimacing against the pain, he heaved himself up out of the twisted tangle of brush and staggered back onto the trail, while the maddened cicadas bounced off his body like toy arrows pinging off metal armor. He shook his head to clear the fog of the collision and steadied himself. He took a deep breath and started off again, his legs churning under him with desperation.

The trail narrowed and rose sharply. Up ahead, about three hundred yards, Lanny saw Carmen's black hair bouncing along her shoulders. Her strong strides pushed her up the trail past clumps of Three-Leaf Sumac that bristled with red berries.

"CAR—!" Lanny was able to get out the first part of her name before he gasped for breath.

Lanny could tell by her determined pace that she was trying to get away from him. This steeled Lanny's resolve and he lowered his head and pumped his legs for all he was worth.

She can get as far away from me as she wants, Lanny thought to himself, *but first I'm going to have my say. And that guy, well, the hell with him.* And Lanny clenched his fists in anger. *If I have to punch him out to get to her I will.*

Lanny's breath came out harshly as he increased his speed. After a minute, Lanny caught sight of Carmen a hundred yards or so ahead of him. With his heart about to burst out of his chest, Lanny sucked in a huge breath and sprinted up the trail in one last kick, his mind echoing with his own words over and over: *I love her. I love her. I love her...*

Suddenly the trail leveled off and headed off into an open Alpine meadow. Lanny could see Carmen about fifty yards ahead of him. Lanny's sprint swallowed the distance between them. His eyes searched for the man but couldn't find him. He must be way out in front of Carmen or maybe he's waiting behind that hillside that jutted into the meadow.

"Carmen!" Lanny yelled after her. "Carmen! Stop! Stop for God's sake!!!

Carmen turned and saw how close Lanny was. Her jog turned into a sprint.

"No! You stop!" Carmen replied breathlessly.

"Carmen! Damn it!" And Lanny forced the last bit of strength he had left in his legs and put on a burst of speed to overtake her.

If I don't catch her now...she's gone. I can't push it anymore. I'm going to drop any second!!!

Lanny closed the gap between them and reached out for Carmen's shoulder.

"Carmen," Lanny panted. "I love—." At that moment the ground went out from under them as the trail suddenly dipped into an abrupt swale. Carmen squealed and Lanny barked out in surprise. They both went tumbling down and sprawled out together in the Indian grass, gasping for breath, chests heaving.

"What the hell did you say, you fool?" Carmen managed in a strained voice while untangling herself from Lanny's arms.

Lanny rolled over on his hands and knees, trying to catch his breath, and looked at Carmen who squinted at the sight of the drying blood on the side of his face. Lanny could feel a knot gathering over his right eye.

"Who the hell is that man with you?" Lanny puffed out. Carmen's eyes flashed. "That's none of your business."
"You're right," Lanny shot back, "but I'm making it my business, damn it."

"Oh," Carmen taunted, "you have a temper. Do you want to fight with him?"

"Don't be ridiculous. I'm no Latin macho."

"Too bad," Carmen sounded disappointed, "it would have been very entertaining. I think—"

"All right," Lanny cut in angrily, "if I had to fight him to have my say, I would. Go ahead, call for him. He, too, can listen to what I have to say. Go ahead, damn it."

Carmen studied Lanny for a moment, her marble black eyes full of light.

Lanny could see she was calculating something. He hoped she couldn't tell that he was almost ready to squirm under her gaze. He expected *that* look any moment now.

"That man was my brother, Manny. His house is over that way," she pointed a long sinuous arm tapered with muscle tone. "He took the trail to Atalaya at the bottom of the canyon. We've been walking in these mountains since we were kids."

Carmen noticed the blood on the side of Lanny's face and the lump above his eye. Her eyes narrowed as if to dismiss a thought.

"What happened to your face?" She began, annoyed.

Lanny put a finger to the lump above his eye and realized how much it was starting to hurt.

"When I started to chase you, I fell into a piñon thicket down at the bottom of the canyon."

Carmen shook her head like a glossy black mare that didn't want to be bridled. Again, annoyed: "You are clumsy. How can you be a tennis pro?"

A tight grin almost turned into a laugh. "I'm not a tennis pro, but you never know. Boy, would my old man have a laugh at that."

"Now, what is *your say* that you have to have? Be quick about it. I have to finish my hike and—"

"Well, if you have to know I—"

"I don't have to know anything from you," Carmen cut in, her voice rising. "Do you think—"

"I love you," Lanny began, defiant. "*That's*…my say. I don't…care…if you think I'm a fool or not…Well, maybe I am. So what?"

Carmen's eyes again flashed. "One stupid kiss and you're in love with me?" She accused.

Lanny shook his head and smiled. "You don't get it, do you? It wasn't the stupid kiss…It was…the time in the indoor courts when I opened my eyes and saw you looking down at me, your hair brushing my face. I loved you then and I didn't even know your name. But even then, my heart knew enough, as much as is does now, Carmen."

"Oh, you are such a fool," she said lowly, her gaze softening with her own feelings; feelings she was just now allowing herself to have, and the intensity of them shook her soul. Her eyes grew moist with truth.

"But, you're just a gringo," she said slowly, her heart not into it.

"So I am. And your Dad likes me."

Lanny reached out his hand, the same way he did when he had lifted up her chin to kiss her on that fateful night.

"Can you love a fool...and a gringo like me?"

As Carmen slowly nodded her head Lanny pressed his lips to hers and they lay back down desperately holding on to one another, an embrace of two heated hearts, two peaceful tears, two longing dreams, and two desires as rich and elemental as the alpine meadow beneath them.

Believe me, part of the joy that comes from playing competitive tennis is being able to face your fears; to be able to deal with the absolute honesty of match play. Man, there is no other crucible like it. But the real value of it is when you are able to take that willingness to face your fears, that willingness to accept the judgment of competition with you into your life beyond the hard lines of the court.
—Lanny Bedford, "The Long Hard Court"

Presently, a young voice cleared itself and spoke above the conversational din in the packed Ford Aerostar van: "What it comes down to is we suck. That's all: we suck."

All the men stopped talking as if on cue and craned their heads towards Junior who slumped down in his seat under the glare of his teammates' stares.

"I'll be damned," Rocky growled, "did you guys just hear what Junior said?"

"Well," Carl said at last, "We haven't really considered that, have we?"

A muscle worked along Rocky's jaw. "The kid has got it wrong. We don't suck. Playing 3.0 sucks."

"Anyway," Junior piped up again, "my old man saw the match and that's what he said, that we suck and believe me, my old man is never wrong."

Alex pulled on his mustache. "I for one don't think that's true. Me and Rocky have played with some of the guys on the 3.5 team and we have beat them more than a few times."

"They couldn't handle my serve, could they partner?"

Alex nodded his head. "That's right."

The van made its way through the winding roads that led to the Picuris Pueblo. The countryside throughout New Mexico (as it seemed, Carl noted) was a place where the elements prevailed: craggy shadowed buttes, distant shelves of plateaus, the harsh and barren red dirt with patches and clumps of stubborn piñon and cedar, their roots stuck like claws into the desperately dry earth, and every now and then, a brave cloud as bright as a cotton ball rolled across the stark and measureless blue sky.

"Who knows? We might suck," Pete Fuentes said flatly while he brushed back a thick lock of salt and pepper hair from his chiseled forehead. "But I don't think any one of us wants to have another experience like that on the court with those old geezers."

"Yeah, who needs it? I sure as hell don't," Tom Tolson blurted out in his usual tense, fidgety manner, his eyes growing bigger behind his thick lenses.

"Mr. Bottom Line is probably right," Bodin drawled.

"So, what the hell are we doing going to an Indian reservation? We could have saved ourselves a lot—" Rocky gestured with both hands.

"We're being polite," Carl cut in firmly while he navigated a sharp turn. "It's the least we can do. We got Herman to agree to play on our team and now we're going to quit on him so the least we can do is to just accept his hospitality, be nice, eat some food, and go home."

"Food. Yeah, I'm starved," Rocky said cheerfully.

"Starved?" Buddha said full of ironic disbelief. "You just had a green chile cheeseburger that you made us stop for back in Espanola."

"I hardly ever get to eat fast food," Rocky answered plaintively, looking around for support.

"Hey Carl," Bodin began, "don't you think Coach is going to be disappointed in us? I mean, we're quittin' on him, too. Aren't we?"

Carl took one hand off the wheel and scratched behind his right ear as he thought for a moment.

"Oh, I suspect he thought this was going to happen. He knew a lot of us didn't want to play at 3.0 anyway."

"Well, I sure as hell would rather get my ass kicked playing 3.5 than 3.0, wouldn't you, partner?"

Buddha pursed his lips and nodded thoughtfully. "Sure would, but I don't think we would get our asses kicked at 3.5 like we did on Sunday. Man," Buddha almost shuddered at the memory, "I was ready to quit tennis altogether after that."

"Yeah, screw it," Tolson said fiercely under his breath, his eyes bulging.

"Anyway, I don't think the coach will be surprised. He knew that this league stuff was new to us and he was right: we didn't know what to expect." And Carl looked in the rearview mirror and saw the men nodding their heads.

"I'll say," Rocky blew the words through his lips. "We didn't expect to have a bunch of Lawrence Welk groupies pull our testicles off one by one and hand them to us. Yeah, we didn't expect that."

*Of all the characteristics that reveal who we are, our habits are the most telling. And that is also true on the tennis court. Winning at tennis is a habit shaped by expectations, desire, a work ethic, concentration, and supreme confidence. The latter being the most important. A pack of wolves all seem the same except for **that** one whose attitude shows he expects to be the boss. For many, winning is a brief string of good luck, a few good bounces, God's will etc. The consistent winner and champion's secret is simply doing what comes naturally.*

—At The Public Courts: Conversations with the Professor, alias the "Pusher."

"Act like you would if you were in a white man's church," Herman responded to Carl's question and grinned.

"Ok," drawled Bodin, his voice skeptical, "I guess we can do that, except I would never go to church in the nude."

"Now there's a thought," Rocky chimed in, voice mischievous as he struggled to remove his shoes. "After that my wife would never bug me to go again."

"We must hurry," Herman said, "my cousin will be here any moment and we all have to be inside. The fire has already started and the rocks have been heated."

"Come on, Tolson," Alex barked out.

Tolson stood there fidgeting, his big eyes looking uncertain.

"It's all right, Tom," Carl soothed, "we're all in this together."

Tolson looked around at the naked men in the last light of dusk that outlined the bodies of the men like cartoon stick figures, some cupping their genitals against the cool wind blowing down off the mountains above them. Unable to suppress his laughter any longer, he put a hand to his mouth and giggled like a kid. This got the attention of all the men because they had never heard Tolson giggle.

"Well, "Rocky said with a laugh gathering in his gut, "who said it was going to look pretty?"

Guffaws all around.

"Well, hurry up, Tom," Bodin managed, his teeth chattering, "I'm about to freeze my nuts off."

Herman gestured toward the sweat lodge that resembled a gigantic beehive—a split cedar frame sunk two feet into the ground and arching five feet high, covered with dark red earth. He pulled back the heavy elk-skin door flap and led the naked men into the lodge. Through the small door opening a shaft of dying light cut across the interior revealing various moving parts of torsos hairy and hairless as the men packed into the small space shoulder to shoulder. Red-hot stones lay in a pit in the center of the room. Carl wrinkled his nose against the onslaught of stale, musty sweat.

"Many in my family," Herman began, his voice whimsical, his lips working in a round yet angular face, "still think of using the sweat lodge not recreationally but as a sacrament, a time for prayer and preparation, for spiritual cleanliness. Also, in the past, in my great grandfather's time, the men would come to the sweat lodge before hunting to purge the body of human odors that might be picked up by a wary deer. Some still take peyote first before the sweat to release any evil from their souls and to help stimulate inner knowledge. And of course the healthy reasons for the sweat are well known. The sweat removes toxins from the body. Viruses and bacteria will not survive in the heat of the lodge. The endocrine glands are stimulated by the rise in temperature."

"Cool," Jr. said lowly. "I'm down with that."

"But also," Herman continued, his tone turning serious as he pulled back on his ponytail, "we are here to think of who we are as tennis warriors, to vision-quest through the steam to what lies ahead of us as men who have come together for a purpose. And when our minds become clean we will connect with the Great Spirit."

Herman looked around in the cloudy shaft of light and sensed some skepticism.

"I can tell you this: whatever your beliefs, the proper respect makes anything possible. No one should be here if they are not ready to be cleansed of such things as anger and jealousy. I know many of us have a lot of anger over what happened last Sunday. I say, open your mind and your heart to see a new way…"

"Herman, I know you mean well," Rocky began politely, "but were talking about tennis and—"

"Open your mind," Herman cut in, his voice steady. "From now on, no talking. Let the silence tell you a thing."

A bulk moved into the opening to the lodge, stuffing out the light.

"This is my cousin, Hoskie," Herman said in the suddenly still darkness. "He will help guide us."

Hoskie's darkened figure paused, then moved through the opening and sat down cross-legged next to Herman. A shaft of light played on his square forehead as it knotted then relaxed into serene concentration. The men became quietly fascinated. They all heard the breathy guttural utterance and then the elk-skin flap was lowered. Total black darkness enveloped them.

The men sat in the pit-like blackness, the silence massing around them. Carl couldn't see the hand that he was holding up two inches before his face, only the dull, glowing rocks. And Carl realized that once his vision was gone he felt that—involuntarily—his other senses began to sharpen. He keenly felt how the heat from the radiating rocks baked his skin and he actually felt how beads of sweat bubbled up from under his skin to surface and run down his temples. He thought he could hear the breathing of each individual man and the wind that blew up against the lodge searching for a hole to enter. He felt the rough and smooth texture of the bark floor under him and the exact amount of pressure he felt from Rocky's shoulder as they were pressed together in the cramped space.

Suddenly, a loud crack startled the silence as Hoskie poured a brew of water, cedar and piñon needles onto the red rocks. A nearly unbearable rush of hot vapor blew over the men and then quickly subsided, leaving in its wake a soft, pleasant odor of burned needles.

Herman's voice told the men: "Only needles from trees struck by lightning can be used on the rocks. The smoke is medicinal. Inhale it. Now drink it—it makes you well."

A wooden bowl was passed around.

Carl pressed the bowl to his lips and sipped the resinous brew as Hoskie began a chant that Herman later told him was to call on Greater Powers to bring strength and luck to the men, to bring courage to them as warriors and hunters.

Rocky thought Herman's little story about the sweat lodge was a bit silly but when Hoskie began his chant it startled his mind and he became absorbed in the sounds, the hair rising on his neck while Goosebumps rose up on the sides of his arms despite the heat.

Alex thought: *Wow, this is some real shit. Whoa, man...*
I'm down. I'm down, Jr. thought over and over.

Bodin and Pete thought: *I'm sweating like a pig.*

Tolson felt his eyes get as big as some nocturnal monkey as he strained his eyes to see through the blackness as if he wanted to see if he was still where he thought he was.

Hoskie continued his impassioned chant and all the men, though not understanding the words, knew in their own ways that an ancient narrative was being told and they were enraptured, each with different feelings and images. The sounds poured through the men as sweat poured from their bodies.

Finally, Hoskie's chanting trailed off into a whisper, leaving the men to believe that the whisper was meant for each one of them....And then Hoskie doused the red rocks with a large splash of brew and another blast of steam assaulted the men and their consciousness. The rocks hissed and sputtered. The steam lingered and drifted through the darkness.

A few moments of deep silence went by.

Herman then said: "Whoever wants to speak can do so, but do so with an open heart."

Silence.

"I'm a coward," the men heard Rocky whisper.

Silence.

"I'm a coward," Rocky whispered again. "If we quit now, we all are."

The whisper seemed to echo through the lodge and the men sat still, absorbing Rocky's words.

Silence.

"I didn't do what Coach said to do," Carl had to admit, his words sinking into the men the way the steaming heat penetrated their skins. "I wasn't a good partner. I played selfishly and I got down on myself. I was a bad partner."

"I didn't trust my partner," came Tolson's tense admission. "I tried to take too many balls because I thought Jr. couldn't get them. I thought I was trying to help but really I didn't trust Jr." Softening: "I'm sorry, Jr."

"I kept thinking how I thought that Rocky was playing like shit and I got so easily disappointed, I couldn't try and encourage and support him better. Hell," Alex spat out disgustedly, "I'm sure I was playing like shit too."

"You were," came Rocky's reply, his tone sympathetic and all the men chuckled in mutual self-deprecation.

"I see it this way," Herman began, "we are either going to be warriors because we fight for the team and for each other, or we're just going to be players with no tribe, no brotherhood." Carl could feel the men all nodding their heads in the blackness.

"I might sound like a sissy," Rocky growled, "but you know, I just realized that I really love the idea of playing with you guys on a team and I will be sorry when it's over."

"We always suspected that you were a sissy," Bodin drawled out.

"Let me tell you what we Indians believe," Herman said through a grin his white teeth shining briefly in the darkness, "the bond between warriors, between men who hunt wild game together or who hunt for victories on the tennis court together, this is not something for sissies."

Herman threw another bowlful of liquid on the rocks and the men felt the scalding blast of the rising steam for a few searing seconds but then they all felt cleansed.

Rocky asked: "Hey, Captain Carl, now that we've decided to continue, who is next on the schedule?"

Carl let out a painful chuckle. "We might want to reconsider our resolve. It would be the Duke City Golf and Racquet Club. The best of Albuquerque. They've been to sectionals the last three years. To say that they're the dominant team is almost an understatement. The guys on our club's 3.5 team told me that they went down there to play and somehow messed up the date and the Duke 3.5 team wasn't there. But their 3.0 team was practicing. Our guys asked them if they wanted to have a practice match. So they decided to play and our guys got smoked five zip."

"Holy shit!" Pete exclaimed. "A bagel?"

"That's right."

"Damn," thought Jr. out loud, "How could we do any better?"

"We couldn't do any worse that's for sure," Carl replied.

Silence filled the primordial blackness as the men were left with their own thoughts. Sweat tickling out through pores could be heard. The dull red glow of the rocks drew the focus and contemplation of the men.
Silence.

"Herman," Carl said finally, his voice deep with conviction, "you said that these sweats are for vision-questing."

"That's correct. It's not unusual for—"

"Guys," Carl cut in on Herman, his voice tinged with excitement, "I think I just had a vision."

"That's a good omen," Herman intoned.

"We're all teammates, right?" Carl asked

"Right," the men replied, their voices coming together in the darkness.

"But most importantly, as we have found out tonight," Carl continued, his voice becoming mysterious, "that we are warriors together…right?

"Right."

Suddenly, a high-pitched, crying chant broke out from Hoskie who had been sitting quietly. He threw a quick splash of liquid on the glowing rocks. All the men felt the hair on the back of their necks rise in unison despite the flush of the stifling heat wave. The chanting was abruptly cut off with a guttural flourish.

"Then," Carl said quietly in the gathering silence, "we must do what warriors would do."

Despite all of the self-help mumbo-jumbo, all of the psychobabble,
all the religious guarantees—there is no escaping this essential
fact: life is like one long unfinished tennis match. Who the hell
cares about the previous point and who the hell cares about the
*points to be? The point you are playing **now** is the only point that*
should ever, ever matter.

—Lanny Bedford, "The Long Hard Court"

"Too bad about your boys, Lan," John said as he toweled
off his face. "I thought they were pretty gung-ho."
Lanny looked up the mountain that towered over the club. The
thinning mantle of snow that had covered the uppermost top of the
mountain during the spring had melted off. Deep green patches of
Aspens dotted the mountainside, interspersed with Colorado blue
spruce, Ponderosa Pine, and Douglas fir, a tapestry of trees that ran
down the mountain and into a uniform forest of piñon.

Lanny said: "I thought I had prepared them, given them an
understanding of what to expect from match conditions and so
forth. I guess I didn't do my job. A voice all along told me that this
would happen. They didn't believe me. Boy, were they
shocked…Oh, well…."

"Nah, you did a good job with them. I saw you. You
worked them hard, showed them a lot of stuff I would have never
shown them. Come on, Lan, you're a natural and you know it. You
weren't just hitting balls with them or just drilling, you were really
teaching, teaching them how to think about a point, the score, the
situation, how to help themselves, to problem-solve with their
partners. I mean," and John flashed his big-toothed grin, "you were
teaching them ah, ah—"

"A craft," Lanny broke in as he downed a cup of water
from the courtside cooler.

"Yeah," and John laughed, "That's it. You were treating
them like artists or something. Dude, you're too much."

"Tennis *is* a craft, my hammer-headed friend," Lanny shot
back with a sly grin.

"Jeez, I say hit the frickin' ball hard and win one more
point that your opponent," John said with a fierce look on his face.

"That's why you're a meat, a meathead on the court with a club in his hands."

Lanny felt something and looked over to the workout room that stood up above the court and saw Carmen waving at him from the window, her shinny dark eyes locked on to his.

Even the wave of her hand is sensual! Lanny thought as his heart leaped in his chest as it always did when he saw her. Lanny waved back.

"Boy oh boy," John began in mock dismay. "You two just can't get enough of each other. Man, get some perspective, will you?"

Lanny looked at John with a you-don't-get-it look and then glanced back to the window where Carmen gazed at him with obvious love. Lanny spoke while his eyes made love to her:

"Mine eye hath play'd the painter and hath stell'd

Thy beauty's form in table of my heart;

My body is the frame wherein 'tis held,

And perspective it is best painter's art..."

"Who the hell said that?" John asked puzzled by the words.

"That was Shakespeare my hammer-headed friend, and of all people, he knew about love's perspective."

John got up off the tennis bench and grabbed his racquet.

"Well, who the hell would have thought that the Dragon Lady would have fallen for you, let alone any man? Dude, you're awesome. Does she still insult you?"

Lanny smiled. "Not as much. But I kind of like it. It's like verbal foreplay."

"Whoa, you're in deep. Deep...Hey, speaking of insults, I think your game has really fallen off. In the Juniors, I could never get a set off you because like you said: I self-destructed. But I've gotten a set the last three times we've played and now, getting to the third set and up a comfortable break, I think it's time to put all those losses behind me. I'm like Vitas Gerulaitis, nobody beats me forty-some-times in a row. You're going down, my man. This will prepare me for the 1992 National 40's tournament in

Albuquerque," John said grinning broadly. "It's a Tier One National Tournament. All the biggies will be there."

Lanny picked up his racquet, feeling the weight fall into his hand like the familiarity of a sword coming out of a well-worn scabbard.

"I'll let you win if you need to feel good about your game going into the tournament. I can appreciate that," Lanny smirked.

"Not a chance bookworm-boy," John flashed his teeth. "The time is now, after all these frickin' years. Now. My time is now. After I beat you I'm going to beat that bastard who I've lost to in the finals for the last four years. Man, I hate losing to a prick."

"Ah, a real nemesis, eh?" Lanny grinned.

"Yeah, you could say that.

"Good player, eh?"

"I guess you could say that," John replied sarcastically. "He has been the number one ranked player in the nation in the 30s, 35s, and now the 40s. Nobody can beat the guy. He was on the tour for about ten years. He's the Director of Tennis at the Duke City Golf and Racquet Club in Albuquerque. A real cocky son-of-a-bitch. Mr. Gold Ball himself."

"Why can't you beat him?"

"He's tough I tell you. But damn it, I've had my chances. I'm right there and then *poof,* the match just slips through my fingers."

Lanny put his forefinger and thumb to his nose, thought for a moment. "So, it's mental. You get mental with him."

John clenched his jaw. "Hey, he puts a lot of pressure on you with his consistency. He plays from the back. I play from the back. We've got the same type of game and he's just better at it than I am."

"No, you're just mental," Lanny insisted.

"Well, if you got off your complacent ass and played a few tournaments I bet you we would see you get mental."

"I never got mental. Besides I don't need to play any tournaments. Been there, done that. I've enjoyed getting back to the court and trying my hand at teaching. That's enough."

I Should lay it on him, John thought quickly. *I could...but not now. No, not yet. But damn, he's pissing me off.*
Agitated, John tapped his racquet on the net cord.

"Enough? I never thought I would hear you say that. That's not the Lanny I remember. Look, if you're afraid to challenge yourself on the court don't go judging me, calling me mental, when you're not out there competing."

Lanny laughed off John's remarks. "That's all pretty funny. Look, I've got nothing to prove. You're being defensive just makes my case. If you're mental about playing some guy just admit it. Mental. So what? Just deal with it."

All right that's it! He's asked for it now. John finally decided and he slapped his racquet down hard on the net cord.

"Oh, Yeah? Deal with it like you dealt with losing in the finals at Kalamazoo? That loss kicked your ass out of tennis. You let a lot of people down, not just your old man. Talk about *mental.*
"

Lanny began to lift up his hand to gesture but John's words pushed back his hand like some blunt force. He felt the muddy bottom of his river start to churn. He licked his suddenly dry lips.

"That was then. I was young. I didn't know what I wanted."

"So you were mental then. So what? Just deal with it," and John looked right into Lanny's eyes, the muscle along his jaw working.
Lanny matched John's stare then a smile started at the sides of both of their mouths and they burst out laughing.

"Yeah, all right, John, all right," Lanny said through chuckles, realizing that the churning had stopped. "Enough with the damn mental stuff already. Look, Kalamazoo notwithstanding, I'm just an ex-champion with an ex-champion's attitude. I admit it. But, I want to help you beat this bastard. And I know how."

"How?"

"You've got to come in more and—"

"But that's not my game. I have to out hit him from the baseline and—"

"That's not going to win it for you and you know it. Look, you've been playing tennis your whole life, you can volley, you can chip and charge and put the pressure on this guy. I know you can. I always thought that if you could have just played more of an all court game—with your speed—you would have beaten me more times than I care to imagine. So let's play some and work on you getting in to the net. That's my game and I sure as hell know how to teach it."

"Shit, Lan, I don't come to net until it's time to shake hands, you know that."

Lanny tapped John's racquet head with his. "Look...That's all in the past, my hammer-headed friend. You're going to find out what you've been missing all these years: the way the game was meant to be played: beautiful violence my old man used to call it and he was right."

"Serve and volley?" John blurted out.

"Why not try some of that?"

"Oh, Lan," John tried to protest, "I'm too old for that shit, I—"

"Oh, come on. Yeah, you're an old fart all right," Lanny mocked. "Hey, you're a tennis player. Serve and volley, chip and charge, smash and crash—it's all a part of the game, that's all." I'll try but I don't know."

"All right let's get started. I'll play like this guy does and we'll get you to pick your spots to get in. A big part of being *mental* about somebody is that you're limited on the court. If you have an all-court game then you have many ways to attack someone."

"I'm not mental about this guy, ok?" John said stubbornly, an edge of anger in his voice.

Lanny ignored John's tone and continued on.

"Ok, ok, don't be so sensitive. I understand. You're not mental with this guy. He just has your number.
John nodded, accepting the characterization. "Yeah, that's right."

"So, I need to be this guy," Lanny said over his shoulder as he walked to the baseline. "What the hell is this bastard's name?"

John had been waiting for this moment, waiting for the right time and he knew he couldn't have a better one.

"His name is Justin Lucchi," John said loudly his voice flat. "We used to call him 'Just Out' because of the way he called the lines in a tight match.

The sound of the name stopped Lanny in his tracks as if one more step would plunge him into a sickening fall over a steep cliff and down onto the jagged rocks below. His face drew in tautly, the sound of the name hanging in the air like a tossed grenade.

"Oh really?" Lanny said strangely, his voice sounding like someone else's.

"The same."

"Really?"

"Yep. That's him. But I thought you had forgotten him." Lanny didn't turn around to look at John because he didn't want him to see how he was fighting to relax his face and still his beating heart. *Come on, that's all past...All in the past.* Finally, Lanny turned, his face calm.

"I really had but now that you've brought him up, well, yeah, I remember him: skinny kid, with the arrogant face, the lobber from hell; he'll hook you on break point. Yeah, Lucchi."

"You're right on all counts. But he's not as skinny anymore, but he still has that arrogant face. He knows he's going to win and that bugs me."

"All right," Lanny said flatly," to hell with that guy. Let's get you figuring out how to beat that bastard and wipe that look off his face. We're going to start with some chipping and charging. I want you to climb all over his ass."

My mom was never around to tell me that there would not only be days like this but…years. And she never told me about that damn muddy river bottom. Damn…
—Lanny Bedford, "The Long Hard Court"

I could, Lanny thought to himself, *lay my head on Carmen's breasts forever. God, what a refuge. To hear the steady beat of her heart; to feel the velvet softness of her skin on my cheek. And now all I can think about is that damn Lucchi!*

"What are you thinking about?" Carmen asked in a whisper. "You got so quiet."

Reluctantly Lanny sat up in bed and tried to see through the darkness of the room to the mirror on the wall, but he didn't need a mirror to see the look on his face. He could feel his past turn full circle under him like a queasy jolt of motion sickness.

Why? Why is it happening now? The past should just stay past. Shouldn't it?

Carmen could sense Lanny was struggling with something. She reached out a smooth arm and caressed his neck.

"Lanny, what's the matter? You've been quiet."

"Nothing, babe," and Lanny grabbed her hand and kissed it.

Carmen brushed her foamy black hair off her forehead in a manner Lanny always liked.

"I guess I've been quiet tonight, too."

"Now that I think of it," Lanny replied, "you have been quiet. I guess I've been a little preoccupied and I didn't notice. I'm sorry, baby." And Lanny kissed her hand again.

"Have you ever been afraid, I mean, really afraid?" Carmen asked almost suddenly, and her words filled the darkness around them and her tone disturbed Lanny.

"What are you getting at?" Lanny asked, trying to keep the alarm out of his voice and then quickly tried to lightened things up. "Well I guess I could say that I was afraid of you?"

"Me?" Carmen asked, surprised." Hell, I was afraid of you," Carmen said in a quick admission.

"Me?" Lanny replied, equally surprised. "Me? You mean I scared you?"

Lanny could see Carmen nodding her head on the pillow.

"Man, I thought you considered me to be some annoying gringo that you couldn't be bothered with."

"You were annoying…but I didn't realized then that I liked your annoying ways," Carmen said through a smile. She turned onto her side and Lanny could see the serious look return to her face in the gray shadow that lay across her profile.

"I had a…a white boyfriend once," Carmen began as if wanting to get the words off her back.

Right away Lanny wanted to let go of all the questions that surged to his lips but he felt it best to let Carmen have her say.

"I can tell you are totally surprised."

"Boy, you can say that again."

Carmen gathered her thoughts and raised herself up on one elbow.

"I was young, off at college, naïve, seduced by his whiteness I guess you could say. I had only dated Hispanic guys before. He was very, very smart, came from a wealthy family. He pulled me into his Anglo world, friends, dinner parties. I got swept up. It was like being in a fantasy and then…and then…he hurt me. All of a sudden he was very dangerous and I felt vulnerable…so vulnerable. I never want to feel like that again, so it was just easy for me to consider all men…you…dangerous. So, I was afraid of you."

"And for my own reasons," Lanny said softly, "I was afraid of you."

"Boy," Carmen said at last, "we sure are a couple of scaredy-cats."

"Oh, baby," Lanny bent down and hugged Carmen tightly. "The thought of someone hurting you makes me sick. I'm not just sounding macho, but I won't let anyone harm you. Believe me," Lanny said his voice tightening with emotion.

"I believe you and I love you and I did before you tackled me on the trail," Carmen flashed a quick smile. "Fear was just getting in the way. Damn that fear. I'm glad that I'm finally able to tell you about it. Boy, what a burden."

"It's all right, baby," Lanny reassured her.

"I know," Carmen said softly as she sighed and lowered herself back down onto her side.

Silence began to languidly fill in the space between them. Lanny looked out into the gray/black gloom of the bedroom, heard a dry branch scratching faintly at the window next to the bed, and his mind returned to the same preoccupation he had had all day.

Presently Carmen said: "What's the matter, honey?"

"I guess I can't sleep."

Carmen put on her haughty commanding tone, a tone they now joked about.

"Well, I command you to lie down and sleep. Now do it."

Lanny smiled. "Ordinarily, I would do whatever you command and I will. I'm just going to get up for a few minutes. I'll come back to bed soon."

"Make sure you do. You don't want to piss me off," she said softly as her fingers moved along the outline of Lanny's goatee that ran sharply down the sides of his mouth and settled under his chin giving his mouth and jaw that masculine, chiseled look.

"Imagine that," Lanny replied through a small laugh as he bent down and kissed Carmen.

Wow, Lanny couldn't help but think to himself as he looked into Carmen soft eyes that made him want to squeeze her and merge his skin with hers: *God, how lucky I am to have her in my life. Everything's great but ... damn ... damn that Lucchi and damn my fears.* He smiled again, hungry as ever to see her smile in return.

"I'll be back in a few."

"All right, baby," Carmen said drowsily and curled herself up like languid cat.

Lanny wandered into the living room. He could still smell the faint odors of piñon smoke, boiling posole, roasted green chiles and pungent red chile that had permeated the adobe walls and the vigas that stretched across the ceiling.

He took down the leather box from the bookshelf and set it on the kitchen table. He poured himself a glass of full-fruited, smoky cabernet. He sat down at the table and opened the box, and the voice of the old professor sounded in his ears.

"My name is Burns. Everyone calls me Professor Burns. And you, my hard-hitting young man?...."

"....My opponents don't realize how much ferocity and aggression lies behind my pushing...When you get beat by me it's not just that I have defeated you...I have punished you..."
Lanny smiled tightly and nodded. *Could I...could I face this fear?* He tried not to ask himself. *I don't really have to. Carmen is with me. My life is getting better. I have something to look forward to. I don't need it. I don't,* he convinced himself, his hands balling into fists.

He gathered up the professor's letters and then read through them as if looking for an answer until the first lights of dawn crept through the shades in the window.

Yes, you can play tennis, but I'm talking out the experience of tennis. Let me tell you—and believe me only a few understand what I mean—when you feel the ball on your strings and it feels more like a caress than a hit, more like love than aggression, more sensual than just physical, then, and only then, can you know what I've known to be the deepest essence of tennis.
—Lanny Bedford, "The Long Hard Court"

"Come on! That's what we want! Come on, meat!!!" Lanny stood up from his seat in the small stadium court and shouted down at John on the court, pumping both his fists and nodding his head vigorously.

John had just hit a big forehand and without hesitation he closed in behind the shot as his opponent, not thinking that John would be in, sliced a defensive floater back which John closed on, putting the volley away. John flashed Lanny a quick but weary grin as if to say: it may be too late.

Lanny almost had to agree. *He should have started doing that early in the second set,* Lanny thought to himself as he cheered John on. *He got the break but I think it's too late and so does Lucchi... that cocky shit,* Lanny almost spat out as Lucchi looked up with his swarthy face accented by a thick muscular nose, overly bright brown eyes, and outlined by short, wire-like salt and pepper hair. He looked at Lanny and they locked eyes, with Lucchi saying: Don't get so excited it's almost over. Lanny knew that arrogant look and he could feel his muscles tense and the frown on his face deepen.

Look at that prick...Yeah, he knows it's too late for John. He's taking his time. Enjoying it. I know that grin! Damn!

John had stayed right with Lucchi in the first set. Long baseline rallies and Lanny still marveled at how fast John was but...*God, this guy Lucchi...what a backboard. Jesus!*

In the first set Lanny thought John could pull it out. Five all and Lucchi was getting a little edgy about all the balls that John ran down, and about the big slappy forehands that John was cranking off for winners. But that big forehand went off a couple of times while John was trying to hold serve. Lucchi spit back a few desperate ones that John tried to hit back even harder. Lucchi hit a few lines, hooked John on a line call that brought Lanny soaring out of his seat amid the jeers from other spectators who were deeply into the match, and that was that. A dogfight up to five all and then that quick break sort of took the wind out of John and the set slipped away. He was still steaming about the call and he lost his concentration and his forehand went off. Nothing was working. All Lanny could think of was how John should be putting the pressure on, getting in behind some of those big forehands that hurt Lucchi.

Man, so few opportunities but he's got to take them.

Lucchi jumped out to a five to two lead in the second set before John looked up and Lanny could read John's lips: "To hell with it, I'm coming in."

He did and that surprised Lucchi. John promptly broke, held serve, broke, and it was suddenly five all. But inexplicably, John stopped coming in. Lucchi held serve and quickly, (almost sickeningly,) got out to Love-Thirty on John's serve after an easy forehand that John simply hit out. And then, John got a mid-court ball, hammered the forehand deep into the corner, but instead of crashing into the net, he hesitated, getting caught in the mid court and Lucchi flicked a desperation shot back just deep and John couldn't return it. Groans filled the stadium court. The next point was a long grueling exchange where Lucchi just counter-punched John to death—again Lucchi gave John that *look* and grin.

Just like that Lucchi had broken John and would now serve for the match.

"Come on, John! Come on!" Lanny shouted almost desperately, an inner fear rising up in him that he had to swallow down before cheering again.

Lucchi looked up into the stands and again locked on to Lanny's eyes and slightly shook his head saying with his gloating expression: it's too late. It's all over.

The last point was brutal. After about the sixth stroke Lanny knew what Lucchi was up to. He was out to punish John. Lucchi knew he had a few points to burn and he was going to move John side to side for as long as he could take it. He wouldn't go for the opening even if he had it, just another ball cross-court hit with just enough pace so that John could reach it and then again back cross court.

He wants John to give up, Lanny thought grimly. *He's toying with him.*

Lanny could hear John grunting with effort running side to side. The crowd gasped with each of John's great gets but Lanny sat, trembling with anger. He swore harshly under his breath. Lucchi's next cross-court ball, the twenty-fourth stroke, sailed just long. Gassed, John barely pulled up before he hit the side fence, sides heaving, his face beet red. John looked up through the fence at Lanny so fatigued that he couldn't manage a smile, but Lanny did hear John wheeze out defiantly:

"One more. One more."

Lanny gave him a brave look and shook his fist at him.

Suddenly, John bent over awkwardly and staggered. The crowd groaned. *Jesus! Cramps!* Lanny's heart leaped with panic. *No, no, John, don't go down. Stay up! Stay up!*

John stiffly righted himself and tried to walk off the cramps. Each time he came back and began to bend down into his service motion the cramps would grab him and again he would try to walk them off.

Lanny saw Lucchi look at the USTA referee who was monitoring the match. Lucchi gestured at the referee as if to say: How long are you going to give him?

The crowd jeered at Lucchi who just shrugged and walked back and got down into his return-of-serve stance. John walked gingerly back to the baseline to serve. Lucchi looked at him and said in a cocky voice:

"Hey John, I know you're hurting. If you want to call it, that's ok. No sense in hurting yourself."

John knew Lucchi was mocking him so he flipped him the finger and the crowd laughed. Lanny sat silent and grim. He started to rethink his vociferous support for John, remembering that match at Kalamazoo against Lucchi, remembering how he had wanted his supporters to shut up and let him just stop; to just let him stop the pain and exhaustion.

Lanny wanted to shout at him: Don't play that bastard's game. You know what he's doing to you. Screw it!

Again, the same kind of point started with John getting pulled side to side and Lucchi with that sly grin on his face.

Damn it, John! Lanny shouted to himself. *That's enough! Don't let him play you like that. Hit the damn ball out!*

Lanny watched as John started to retrieve another cross-court ball. Grunting with effort, John's legs wouldn't go anymore and he pulled up cramping. He went to one knee then down and rolled over on his back in full spasm.
Damn!

Lanny leaped up and rushed down on to the court and quickly reached John who was writhing in pain.
"Come on, Johnny boy, get up." Lanny put both arms under John and lifted him up. "We've got to get you up. I know it hurts. Come on, get up. We've got to walk you."

Lanny put an arm around John's waist and started walking him while John gasped in pain. Lucchi had slowly walked over from his side of the net and said, not a note of compassion in his voice:

"Cramps. That's a bummer." He sniffed. "A real bummer."

Lanny looked Lucchi right in the eye and shot back:

"You know, Lucchi, after all these years, you're still an asshole. And that call in the first set, you still don't know that the fuckin' line is **in.**"

Lucchi gave Lanny a puzzled look trying to place him but couldn't. He shrugged.

"It was close, but sorry, I saw it just out."

"Just out," Lanny spat out sourly. 'Just Out Lucchi.' You're still living up to your nickname."

Lucchi squinted at Lanny failing to recollect him, while ignoring Lanny's comment.

"Do I know you?" he asked Lanny.

Lanny thought for a moment started to say something but said instead as he cocked his head to one side: "No, but I know who you are."

"Oh well," Lucchi said with an air of nonchalance. He gestured at John who clung to Lanny's shoulder.

"Tough break, John. Sorry."

"Fuck off, Lucchi," John managed in a pained voice.

Lucchi smiled, chuckled to himself and walked off saying: "Next."

Lanny helped John off the court and grabbed John's tennis bag as they passed the bench.

"There's a grassy area over there with some trees," Lanny said.

John gasped again as a cramp gripped his thigh. He came to a rigid stop.

"Come on," Lanny encouraged. "Walk it off. There you go. Here, chug down some of this water."

They walked around the shady area.

John took a deep breath and the cramps started to subside.

"Meat, "Lanny began, "I was real proud of you."

"You were?"

"The way you were coming in there for a couple of games really stopped Lucchi's momentum and it allowed you to get back into the game."

"But I got away from it at the end there," John said dejectedly. "I had the bastard. I just got pissed when he hooked me. I knew that was going to happen. I was prepared for it but it got to me. Damn! And then at the end he toyed with me. Worked me over good."

"You were always a fighter. You did good. It took courage to come in and take the net. Next time it'll be easier for you."

A loud speaker from the tennis desk called out: "L.B. McNulty and Cruz Sanchez next on stadium."

Lanny turned to go.

"Where you goin?"

"That's me," Lanny said.

"You?" John blurted out in surprise. "You're playing?"

"Yeah," Lanny nodded. "L.B. McNulty. Lanny Bedford McNulty. McNulty was my mother's maiden name. You told me that I had no right to accuse you of being mental with Lucchi if I wasn't out here challenging myself and going *mano a mano*."

"Ah," John said with a sly smile on his face. "So you're the L.B. McNulty guy whose been making his way through the draw. The guy nobody had heard of before. Eric Johnson asked me yesterday if I knew you. Hell, I didn't know it was you. But he sure as hell knows you now. You beat him one and one. He said he got spanked pretty good. Yeah, I'll bet he—."

And John started to laugh but a cramp cut off his amusement.

"Hey take it easy," Lanny said, and started to rub out the cramp in John's thigh.

"Is that a little better?"

"Yeah, it's starting to let go. Yeah, there," and John sighed with relief.

"Here, sit down in this chair and drink a lot of water. Ease down. There. Take this water. I got to go. Are you going to be all right?"

"Yeah, as long as I don't move. So how did you beat Johnson one and one?"

"Well, first two matches I was a bit shaky, some nerves, some hesitation. When I played Johnson my playing instincts were starting to come back to me: I was moving better, earlier, anticipating better, a lot more sure of what I was doing. The ball was feeling good."

John smirked knowingly. "The ball was feeling good. Damn if that ain't the old Lanny I knew. Everybody else would talk about how good their strokes were feeling, but Lanny, no, he would just say some shit about how the ball felt and we would all look at you like you were nuts or something."

Lanny smiled with the memory and then realized that a feeling long dormant within him, something deep under his muddy river was awakening.

"How about this Cruz Sanchez?" Lanny asked.

"Cruz? Well, he played at UNM. Tough competitor. Nobody wants to play him; that kind of guy. He plays at the back, a lot of loopy top."

"Good. I'll see if he can hit that past me."

"Likes to get a rhythm."

"He won't get any," Lanny said as a matter of fact.

"Fairly big first serve but his second serve can be attacked."

"Good. I think I like my chances."

"You going to win?" John asked. "If you do, you get to play Lucchi. It'll be a rematch from twenty-two years ago. Jeez, what a hell of a coincidence. Lucchi, he didn't recognize you, did he?"

"No, why should he? After all he kicked my butt."

"Now I wouldn't say that," John shot back quickly. "One missed volley that's all that was between you."

"Well, as I remember it, he beat me up physically pretty bad."

"Like me today, huh?"

"Yeah," Lanny nodded. "Yeah, just like you today."

"Bastard."

"Yeah, that he is."

Lanny paused, forefinger and thumb caressing his nose.

"Well," Lanny began with a sigh, "I've got to take care of this Cruz guy first and then...and then we'll see. I don't know."

Lanny picked up his tennis bag and walked off.

"What do you mean, '"we'll see?"' John called after Lanny. "Don't get mental on me."

Lanny turned around a tight smile on his face feeling the same fear he had felt during John's match; a fear he now realized was in having to face Lucchi if he beat Sanchez.

"You won't let me forget that, will you?"

Bury my heart under the service line where I took my volley into so many battles.
—Lanny Bedford, Epilogue, "The Long Hard Court"

Lanny couldn't remember waiting so long for a match to begin. Time had detoured into the labyrinth of his past, like a slow motion camera taking a montage of scenes that had shaped him, pained him, renamed him and became a self-movie that made him a refugee in his own heart. All night he lay without the succor of sleep, his eyes dry from their openness, unable to blink back the moving images that tumbled out before his mind and then slipped like evanescent moments into the gloominess of his darkened bedroom. Fear and anger gathered in him and under his skin like an insidious plot.

He was glad that Carmen had to attend a family function. He hardly could have made good company. He didn't tell her he was playing in the tournament. He really wanted to be totally anonymous when he played his first tournament in twenty-one years. John, however, did know but that couldn't have been helped. And certainly he didn't want Carmen to see him get spanked and pushed around by Lucchi tomorrow. He didn't know how he would react and he didn't want her to see whatever he did. Tomorrow was a big mystery except for the…fear and anger.

Finally, finally the match time arrived after Lanny retied his shoes for the twentieth time. He came out of the locker room where he had been pacing for an hour like a restless thoroughbred in a small stall. A lot of spectators gathered in the small stadium court. Already the gossip about Lanny made its rounds and plenty of people were curious because Lucchi, in years past, had never been challenged. They all knew how close John had come so they were all curious about L.B. McNulty, "the new guy."

"Where was he from?" came the question from many people especially from those he had defeated.

"I've never seen him around here. Not at any of the tournaments."

"He's not too talkative," one said dryly.

"Yeah," another agreed, "he just goes about his business. He might be a nice guy. Who knows?"

"What a smooth player," an old wag offered as he took off his tennis cap and ran a thickly veined hand through sparse gray hair. "I saw all three of his matches. He has an old style to him. He kind of glides around and hits the ball without an ounce of effort; reminds me a little of Ken Rosewall, especially that backhand. What a knife. Looked to me like he had played a lot with a wooden racquet. But against Lucchi, I don't know. I think Lucchi will have his way with him. He does with everybody else."

All the men nodded.

"Yeah," agreed a grizzled old court rat, his paunch sticking well over his old short, short, white Rod Laver tennis shorts. "It'll be quick," he added, as he munched on a powdered donut.

During the warm-up Lanny instinctively looked up into the right side of the stadium like he always did before a finals match to lock eyes with his father. He caught himself and shook his head.

What am I doing that for? That was weird. Oh, well, he sighed to himself but couldn't help wondering what the old man would have thought. And Lanny could hear a bitter laugh coming from his father's lips as he started hitting with Lucchi who already had that knowing smirk on his face.

Damn him.

Then Lanny realized that the fear and anger had spread deeply within him and his heart rate was way up. His feet were jittery underneath him and all he could think of was how he wanted to jump all over Lucchi in the first set and smother him and—

Wipe that goddamn smirk off his face!!! And: *Enough with this stupid warm-up. Let's go!!!*

The umpire for the finals came down off his chair and signaled for Lanny and Lucchi to come to the net for the flip. Lanny couldn't help but notice how casual Lucchi seemed, almost with an air of indifference.

"Ah," Lucchi remarked as if really seeing Lanny for the first time, "You're John's friend, aren't you?"

Lanny nodded slightly.

"How is he?"

"He's all right," Lanny said as he squinted into the sun. "He's an old buddy of mine."

"Old John got pretty close this time. But you know, I've never lost to John." A toothy smile spilled out of his mouth. "I guess I've just got his number. Have you ever played him?"

"Many, many times."

"And?"

"I've never lost to John."

"Oh," Lucchi said, and for a moment he lost his indifferent look. Something made him look a little closer at Lanny. He cocked his head to one side and then the look vanished

"Call it," the umpire said.

Lucchi gestured at Lanny with feigned politeness.

"Heads," Lanny grunted.

"Tails," the umpire reported. "Well, Mr. Lucchi?"

Lucchi took a long look at Lanny, his smirk growing bigger.

"Well, Mr. McNulty—can I call you L.B.?"

"Sure," Lanny replied barely moving his lips.

"Well, L.B. you look like you're chomping at the bit so I guess I'll let you have the first crack. I'll return."

Lanny smiled grimly. "Good luck, Lucchi."

"I've never needed good luck," Lucchi shot back with an edge in his voice. "And I know I won't need it now. But you, I think you'll need some; in fact you'll need a lot."

"We'll see." Lanny said through a smile. "And remember, the line is in."

Lucchi grunted sarcastically. "I'm glad you told me. You know, the umpire here, he just calls the score," and Lucchi flashed a broad predatory smile "He lets the players call their own. He figures it's a friendly match," Lucchi's voice mocked, and he turned to walk back to the baseline.

Lanny watched Lucchi walk away and made a mental note to get prepared for the "hook." He picked up the three new balls and instantly felt the heaviness of them because they were designed for high-altitude playing.

I'll never get used to these rocks, Lanny thought. *They're like hitting with a baseball.*

As Lanny turned and walked back to serve he took a moment to glance up into the sun and overheard a couple of spectators commenting on how unusually hot it was. Lanny had seen the heat gauge next to the court. It said ninety-eight degrees.

Lanny had a sudden flashback to Kalamazoo: the boiling heat of the court under his shoes, the dehydration, the merciless sun, the stale, hot air…He shook his head to clear those memories out of his head.

Lanny lifted his hand and Lucchi waved back and Lanny got into his ritual four bounces and his focus suddenly turned inward like air through a vacuum tube. He only faintly heard the bouncing of the ball because his pounding heart drowned out all the sounds around him and he waited for the struggle within him to finish.

He backed off the baseline like a nervous stallion that had just caught the scent of a nearby pack of wolves. He pretended to adjust his hat and took a moment to fiddle with tucking his shirt in and then came back to the line. Again he bounced the ball four times and realized he wasn't going to start out with the feeling of anger that he had wanted. He knew it as he tossed the ball up in the deep blue New Mexican sky: *I'm not angry, damn it…. I'm afraid…*

And his first serve landed way down in the bottom of the net. Lanny realized that he had never swung so hard at a first serve in his life. His hat had nearly come off.

Whoa, now. Wait a second… Just spin it into the body and let's see.

Lanny won a very shaky first game. Because Lanny was the only serve and volleyer in the draw, Lucchi needed to adjust to a net-rusher and so he wasn't able to put his return where he had wanted. Despite missing all of his first serves, Lanny was able to hold, but he knew Lucchi had just probed him and soon, if he didn't get any first serves in, he was going to start seeing the return go by him or down at his feet.

They switched sides and out of the corner of Lanny's eye he could see Lucchi had that look of indifference and that body posture which said he wasn't concerned and that he very much expected to win. It was only a matter of time until he got the rhythm on his return.

And he did.

Lanny was broken quickly in the third and fifth games, had to scrap out some incredibly difficult volleys to get the seventh game, while Lucchi held serve fairly easily and served out the set at 6-2. Lucchi got a lot of first serves in taking away Lanny's chip and charge and once into the rally, Lucchi kept the ball deep, not giving Lanny anything to work with and he won all of the long rallies.

I sure am getting my ass kicked, Lanny thought, berating himself as he and Lucchi walked over to the water cooler. *And to think that I was going to smother him in the first set.*

Lucchi caught brief eye contact with Lanny, sighed, and gave his eyes a slight roll as if saying: tough first set. But Lanny noted the mockery behind the gesture.

Lucchi poured a cup and offered it to Lanny who waved it off and got his own. Lucchi shrugged and casually sipped his water, while Lanny chugged down three quick cups. As Lanny turned to sit down and towel off Lucchi said skeptically:

"So, you've never lost to John?"

Lanny just looked at Lucchi, his blue eyes frosting.

What an asshole, Lanny thought. *He just wants to get into my head, the prick.*

"Hmmm, I find that interesting, L.B.," Lucchi said, with a tone of amusement under each word. "John is a tough, tough player. But like I said: sometimes you've just got a guy's number," Lucchi smiled broadly, again showing Lanny all of his numerous, small teeth.

Lanny took the bait.

"So, you think you've got my number, eh?" Lanny almost spit out the question.

"Judge for yourself," Lucchi replied casually. "Look, serve and volley, well, it's a hard game to win with now-a-days, especially at our level. When you get to be forty, well, it's hard to cover all of the net you need to in order to win. And, Lucchi stopped for a moment to give Lanny a look of ironic sympathy, "if you can't get any first serves in, well it's like target practice for a guy like me. You just have to be really exceptional to serve and volley. When I was on tour I ran into a couple of them, played McEnroe a few times and got a couple of games. But off the tour I only played one serve and volleyer who had McEnroe-like potential but that was a long time ago, in the juniors. But he kind of choked against me and that was the last I heard of him. Hell, I can't remember his name—was it Beresferd, Bereson—something like that. Anyway, serve and volley is a dying style. Sorry." Again the smirk.

When Lucchi said the word "choke," Lanny buried his face in the towel and gave it a vigorous rub, not wanting to let Lucchi see the shock on his face and then the weight of the pain slumping his shoulders.

"Time," the umpire called.

"One more to go," Lucchi said to himself.

Lanny trudged slowly to the baseline, the many-voices of his past beginning to sound off: at first a low muffling of words that began to grow louder and clearer.

You choked!

No, I didn't. I just missed one lousy volley. That's all.

No, you choked. Simple as that. Admit it.

One volley out of a hundred or so. We're talking one volley here.

Admit it. You were scared. Just like you are now....

Lucchi ran off with the first two games while Lanny fought with himself.

What am I doing? Lanny thought meekly to himself. *I should have never come back. Tennis was over for me. OVER. Just like this match. The last match of my—*

"Come on, Coach!" A voice shouted hoarsely from the stands and there was no mistaking who had shouted. "What the hell's going on! We're here to get your ass fired up!!!

Rocky.

A round of laughter made its way around the small stadium court as Lanny looked over at the first row and saw Rocky gesturing at him. The whole 3.0 team was there. Lanny didn't recognize them at first.

"It's too late," came a voice from above Rocky.

"It was too late when it started," one of the old tennis wags leaning against a light pole had to add.

Rocky shot angry glances at the two comments. "Who in the fuck asked you, grandpa?" Rocky barked.

"Calm down, Rocky," Carl said as he grabbed a hold of Rocky's arm to keep him from going over and confronting the old man who realized that Rocky might be a psycho and moved away while looking warily back at Rocky.

Lanny had to go over and retrieve a ball next to the fence where the team was sitting. Lanny finally noticed why he didn't recognize the team. They had...paint on their faces.

Carl couldn't help himself, beaming: "Coach, we gave ourselves a little courage with the paint."

"Yeah," added Tolson, his eyes as big as ever, "Captain Holmes thought we should do as warriors would do."

"We beat that team from the Duke City Racquet Club, the best team in the league! We put on our war paint and—"

"Kicked their ass," Bodin cut in, excitement under his drawl.

"We didn't quit like you thought we did," Rocky added. "Now, don't you quit on us, Coach. Come on," Rocky added fiercely under his breath. And all the men shook their fists in encouragement.

Lanny had to smile at the men, with their war paint still on their faces, flush with victory and a few beers, Lanny could tell.

"Let's go. No talking to the spectators," the umpire said at Lanny while Lucchi gestured at his wristwatch.

Lanny picked up the ball. "I'm happy for you guys."

"We did good, coach?" Carl asked.

"You did real good," Lanny said, adding, "I'm sorry I can't show you guys a better match."

Lanny walked back to the baseline to serve at 0-2 and the men clapped and loudly cheered him on. As he went through his ritual the dialogue returned. He missed the first serve badly. His second was short in the box and Lucchi teed off on it and hammered it by Lanny who had no play and had barely finished his split-step as the return passed him by like a bullet. Lanny visibly slumped his shoulders saying with his body language that there's nothing he could do. Lanny walked slowly back to the baseline. Two bounces, a third, then:

"Come on, Bedford!" a deep voice called out over the quiet, "Don't quit on yourself!"

Startled, Lanny jerked his head up and stopped his fourth bounce. *Dad!*

There was no mistaking that voice he hadn't heard in twenty years.

Dad!

Lanny could see his father, Paul Bedford, sitting next to John and Carmen who looked at Lanny with love in her eyes. John had his large-toothed expression on. His father looked right into Lanny's eyes and Lanny could see the intensity start to gather in his father's expression. Paul Bedford slowly raised both fists as he used to do when Lanny was battling in a big match and shook them, and Lanny could read his lips: "Come on! Don't quit!"…And then the old man gave Lanny a thumbs-up sign, once, then twice. Lanny's mind suddenly flashed back to that moment at Kalamazoo and the twenty years of denial that had burdened his life—all of it past before his mind's eye like a rapid montage. He suddenly jerked backed off from the beginnings of his service motion, and had to push his lips together to keep the words that he was shouting in his mind from bursting out:

All right! I choked! I choked! God, I choked!

Something let go in Lanny and he drew in a deep breath and let out a breath that was heavy with the weight of his past. Again, in…out. And then the feeling surged within him. ANGER.

Yes, anger! Oh, damn, damn! There it is. I wasted my talent. I lied to myself all these years, and this Lucchi, he' going to pay. He's going to pay...

And then a flash of insight struck Lanny as he realized that his father's thumbs-up sign was a message.

Yes! A message! Boy he still knows my game so well. I'm not getting up on my first serve. I'm so anxious to get into net that I'm not exploding up on my serve. Yes! That's it!

Whappp! The ball thundered off of Lanny's strings.

Ace.

Yes, that's it!

Whappp! Another ace.

Lanny could feel a surge of sensation flowing through his body. His hands tingled.

Another first serve in and Lanny closed in behind it and cracked a pure volley deep into the corner for a winner.

The feeling ... it's back. It's back, Lanny thought to himself as he blew tenderly on his hand.

Lanny held serve and he and Lucchi changed ends, while Lanny's team stomped and cheered.

Lucchi sat down on the bench next to Lanny and smirked.

"I see it's getting to be a carnival out here. Remember, a couple of aces won't turn around a match, McNulty."

"The name is Bedford."

A spasm of recognition passed across Lucchi's face.

"You?"

Lanny took a big swig of water wiped his mouth and looked down on Lucchi.

"It's been twenty years since I choked against you. But that was then and now it's time for a little payback... I'm going to kick your ass and I'm going to win this second set playing your game. I'm going to out-hit you from the back and then it'll be over," Lanny said, with a calm conviction, but his eyes were icy.

"Whoa," Lucchi mocked as he stood up. "I guess those twenty years gave you a sense of humor," Lucchi grinned and then a scowl came over his face.

"Beat me from the back? Nobody beats me from the back. Nobody."

The next six games took an hour and a half. Every game went to eight or ten deuces. The New Mexico sun climbed directly above them and beat down on the court with unrelenting heat and brightness. Despite the absence of humidity both men poured sweat. The match had become a war of attrition, of who's going to miss first, with ten to fifteen ball rallies, moving each other from side to side. Lanny's jaw was set. He calmed his instinct to get into net and his anger steeled him to fight along the baseline the way he did at the service line. He put all his focus into his footwork. He was going to get to every ball set up and let his body hit the ball. The score didn't matter; the way the ball came at him in all its variety of spins and paces didn't matter; the only thing that mattered was getting the ball back.

Up in the stands John was almost beside himself that Lanny wasn't serving and volleying and trying to get in to the net at every opportunity.

"Come on, Lan!!! Come on! Play your game! Play your game!!!

John shouted angrily and then had to cheer and pump his fist when Lanny won a grueling backcourt rally. During the changeovers all John could do was jump around in his seat and gnash his teeth with exasperation.

"Mr. Bedford, what the hell is Lanny doing?!" John asked, agonized, almost pulling at his hair. "I've never seen him play this way."

Paul Bedford had sat during the whole set without emotion but watching intently. Twenty years ago he would have been going bananas just like John. But it was time, after all of this time and what had gone on between them, to let Lanny just play and he would just watch, a silent supporter, thinking to himself: *I'm here, son. I'm here for you. I'm here.*

During the set he and Lanny had locked eyes a couple of times each reading the other's mind. Paul saying with his eyes: It's okay, son. It's all right. We're together again. Nothing else matters. And Lanny's eyes flashing relief and saying: This is for you, Dad, for all those years and times you spent with me on the court. I wouldn't trade those times for anything.

Paul reached over and patted John on the forearm and said calmly:

"Relax, John, Lanny knows what he's doing. After all this time, you don't just play a guy who beat you twenty years ago and who pushed you out of the game. No, winning is not enough. You have to prove a special point. Lanny's old coach, Professor Burns, told him once that while it's very risky, sometimes you have to beat someone who appears to be your rival, by playing to their strength even if it's not yours. In that way Professor Burns said, you take a piece of their heart that can never be returned and then you would have their number so to speak, forever. That's what he's doing. I wouldn't have suggested it and it still may fail but I understand, boy, do I understand."

At five all, thirty all, Lanny and Lucchi were deep into a grinding rally when Lanny hit a deep cross-court ball that had Lucchi digging for all he was worth to get to the ball. Just before the ball landed on the line Lucchi yelled a breathless "Out!" Lanny's 3.0 team all jumped out of their seats groaning and crying out in protest, their painted faces contorted with anger and disbelief. Even the two old tennis rats had to look knowingly at each other. They knew Lucchi, too.

John bellowed down from the stands.

"Come on, that's a bull-shit call! Get the umpire, Lanny. Let him call the lines!"

"Yeah!!" almost all the 3.0 men shouted in unison.

Lanny stood, hands on his hips breathing deeply. He took a moment to wipe the sweat out of his eyes.

"You saw that ball, out, Lucchi?" Lanny asked knowing the answer, but he wanted Lucchi to have to lie again in front of the spectators.

Lucchi shrugged. "Sorry, it was just out."

"You're sure?"

"Yep." Came Lucchi's curt reply.

Lanny smiled and said: "Just Out Lucchi."

The spectators who heard Lanny started to chuckle.

"Look, Bedford," Lucchi said angrily, "it was out. I called it out. If you want the umpire to call the lines go ahead and ask for it. I don't care."

"Yeah, Lanny," John said, "let the ump call the lines."

Lanny looked up at John and at the men who were nodding vigorously and then he looked at his dad who let a small grin crease his face and Lanny understood and grinned as well. Lanny looked back to Lucchi.

"No that's all right. Good call...Good call."

"My ad," Lucchi said loud enough for everyone to hear.

For a moment Lanny had to fight down his desire to abandon his plan and to chip and charge Lucchi who hadn't seen Lanny at the net for the entire set. It would be a perfect time to put the pressure on Lucchi to come up with a passing shot. *No, not now.*

Lanny backed away from the baseline as he caught the image of the old Professor leaning against the side fence his fingers sticking through the links and nodding his head, just like he always did when he thought Lanny was doing the right thing.

All right, come on.

Lanny stepped up to the baseline, and as he settled into his crouch, he realized he felt neither anger nor fear...he felt...joy and a centered peace. Joy.

Moving with a fluidity that made his quickness seem slow, he stepped into Lucchi's first serve. The ball appeared to disappear into the middle of Lanny strings and then it flew off down the line for a winner. Lanny's stroke had almost seemed nonchalant. The crowd groaned with awe.

Lucchi took that shot like a body blow and he visibly staggered. Lanny broke on the next point and then served out the set with an ace down the "T."

The stadium erupted with applause. Lanny's 3.0 men were jumping up and down. John and Carmen were on their feet while Paul Bedford sat calmly. He and Lanny locked eyes.

It's time now, Dad.

Show it to me, son.

This time it was Lanny who got to the water cooler first, poured a cup and offered it to Lucchi who angrily waved it off.

"I know how you feel," Lanny said with irony.

"It ain't over, Bedford," Lucchi snarled.

"You can't beat me," Lanny said as a matter of fact. "I just beat you from the back and I know I can beat you by coming in. You're out of options, pal."

"The third set is my option," Lucchi said confidently as he toweled off. "Let's see how fit you are. I know you can't keep up what you're doing. Stay in the back and I'll take your legs out from under you. I promise."

"I can see that you're fit, Lucchi," Lanny said as he fingered his strings, "and I know you think the third set is about who is in better shape. It's hot as hell out here and we're both running low but this isn't Kalamazoo twenty years ago."

"Oh, really?" Lucchi said as a wolfish smile broke out across his sweat-beaded face.

"Time," the umpire called out.

"Sorry," Lanny said as he picked up the three balls from off the tennis caddy, "this set isn't going to be about fitness. It's going to be about skill."

And then it began: a barrage of serves and volleys. Lanny showed everyone a lost art: stinging volleys, sharply angled volleys, half-volleys that had eyes for the line, drop-volleys that dropped onto the court like they were dropping onto a sandy beach, scissor-kick overheads that cracked into the corners like lasers. The applause stopped at 4-0 and everyone watched in fascinated silence, even John marveled at how long the ball seemed to stay on Lanny's strings.

It's like his racquet head is a glove, John thought to himself as he shook his head and looked over at Paul Bedford who merely smiled and they both said at the same time:

"Beautiful violence."

On every second serve that Lanny was returning he would punch a forehand or backhand slice deep in the corner with so much under spin that the ball barely came up, like a grass court bounce, and then smother the net. And he seemed to know which side Lucchi would try to pass on.

Lucchi started to look at Lanny in amazement, the smirk long gone.

I guess I'll never see that again, Lanny thought to himself as he prepared to chip and charge the return of Lucchi's second serve. Lanny had a break point with Lucchi serving down love-4.

Lanny got a little too far under the ball and it popped up a bit into the middle of the court. Lanny knew what was coming as he came into net.

Lucchi got around the ball quickly and wound up with a huge backswing. Lanny could see the rage and anger contorting Lucchi's face as he set up.

He's coming for me.

Lanny relaxed his whole body and prepared to accept anything that came at him. He felt nothing but love for the ball.

The strings of Lucchi's racket exploded and the ball rocketed off and headed straight for Lanny's left hip.

Lanny saw the ball, despite its furious pace, like it was as big as a softball. His mind slowed the ball down and he turned to his right with a fluid twist and stuck his racquet behind and around his back and the ball ricocheted off his strings and passed Lucchi who barely had a chance to see the ball come back.

Cries of amazement and admiration filled the stadium. Lanny's 3.0 guys whooped and hollered. This time Paul Bedford jumped to his feet with John and Carmen and applauded wildly.

Lucchi sagged his shoulders in disbelief. He started to change sides but stopped in midstride. He turned around and then just walked to the net to shake hands. He was done.

"Man," Lucchi had to admit with admiration in his tone, "I've only seen the types of shots you were hitting out there on the tour and some, I've never seen before. You know…twenty years ago you should have beaten me at Kalamazoo. You were the better player. You could have easily played on tour. Top-ten I would have bet anything on it. What happened?

The applause sounded in Lanny's ears. He looked around for a moment, then he looked down at his right hand and knew the alien heaviness that had entered his hand that fateful day would never return.

"What happened?" Lucchi asked again as they walked along the net.

Lanny stopped and turned to Lucchi his forefinger and thumb caressing his nose.

"For me tennis was always, always about loving the ball *and* that indescribable feeling I would get when the ball was on my strings. I lost them both that day because I was young. I didn't realize what that love meant to me, and I wouldn't fight for it. It's all about love, Lucchi."

Lucchi shot Lanny a puzzled look of admiration. "Love?" Lucchi asked, his voice unsure.

Lanny looked up at Carmen's beautiful face, her dark hair waving in the slight breeze and then to his father's nodding face of approval.

"Tennis," Lanny began as he turned his head to look at Lucchi, "and life…it's all about love; it's all about love.

The End

About The Author

Tim Mullane was born in Colorado into a military family. He spent his youth avoiding his Marine Corps Officer father, an experience that inspired his first novel, *Watching the Mudface*. He also authored *Down a Break,* and *The Fire Waits,* the companion novel to *The Piano Mirror's Power.* He attended UCLA where he managed to earn a Ph.D. in History. Tim is an inveterate dreamer, a sometime poet and a life-long writer. For some time he has worked as the Head Tennis Professional for a health club in Bend, Oregon, where he lives restlessly. There's a good chance you might find him on his mountain bike, deep in the Deschutes National Forest spouting off lines of narrative into a hand recorder.